BIG
dreams

Pamela Ann Sun

Published in Australia by
GoGirls Publishing
Address: Suite 2.24 West
4 Ilya Ave Erina NSW
Tel: 02 4326 1338
Email: pamela@pamelaannsun.com
Website: www.pamelaannsun.com

First published in Australia 2017
Copyright © Pamela Ann Sun 2017

National Library of Australia
Cataloguing-in-Publication entry

Creator:	Sun, Pamela Ann, author.
Title:	Big dreams / by Pamela Ann Sun; edited by Anita Saunders
ISBN:	978-0-9954081-2-8 (paperback)
Subjects:	Friendship--Fiction.
	Bildungsromans
	Romance fiction.
	England, South-East--Fiction.

Other Creators/Contributors: Saunders, Anita, editor.

Cover photography by Essence Images
Cover layout and design by Jennifer Burrell, Fresh Vision
Book typesetting by Nelly Murariu, PixBeeDesign
Printed by Griffin Press

Disclaimer

For my amazing daughters.

Praises for *Big Dreams*

Wonderful book! An incredible story of life—being young and fancy free during the 1960's; laughter, friendship, pent up feelings, love, romance, betrayal and sadness. I wasn't prepared for the flood of deep emotions. Memorable characters with personal stories worth exploring. Couldn't put it down.

Julie Postance, Author of *Breaking the Sound Barrier*

If you love all that was associated with the 60's – massive cultural shifts on music, fashion and women's rights, then you'll love *Big Dreams!* After reading the book I wish I could have been there. Fabulous!

Ursula Thompson, Melbourne

I started to read *Big Dreams* and I was so hooked on it that I couldn't put it down. It normally takes me weeks to read a book.

Kath Bateup, Tonbridge

I enjoyed reading my wife's book, *Big Dreams!* It brought back so many memories of Sevenoaks, Tunbridge Wells and Folkestone from my youth. OK, a girly story but wonderfully written. Liked the 'shades' bit!

Tony Carey, Northants

A compelling read. Truthful, absorbing and a heartfelt story. A teenager dreaming of a life of adventure she had all planned out. Loving the music and the fashion pulsating all around her. Freedom and the big world beckoned. What a time to be alive...the 60s. Suddenly everything changed! Did the music stop playing? Oops!

Sylvia Payton, Manly

One

L ily ran to the station, lugging her overnight bag, getting hotter by the minute in the July English sunshine. Rounding the corner into the station drive, she stared into the distance for the black plumes of smoke that would appease her anxiety of missing the train. She knew it was silly; the big, blustering steam trains had been put out to pasture nearly two years ago. She missed the train arriving at the platform, snorting and blowing like an impatient black, majestic steed, ready to carry her away on her journey. There had been soot on the doors but the seats had been tall and well-padded and there had been more space than in the sleek new, electric trains.

As she pushed on, she could see people going through the station door and knew she was in luck. Once on the platform her excitement bubbled up again in anticipation of seeing a live band tonight with her friend Jo. Eager to get on with her day, she had sprung out of bed before eight, whizzed up the hill to the village to work three hours in the fruit shop, then back down the hill and hopped onto a train to Maidstone. With her ten shillings pay, she had bought a fab new Mary Quant-style dress for their Saturday night out. She had barely had time to get back home, pack her bag and get back to the station. Now sitting on the train to Sevenoaks and marvelling at her new weekend freedom, she peeked in her bag, making sure her dress and white stiletto shoes were inside.

A miracle had occurred eight weeks ago when her parents gave into her pleas to stay overnight at Jo's house. Up until then the most that she could hope for was watching *Top of the Pops* on TV on a Saturday night at home. She had quickly learned to stay in a T-shirt and jeans when she left the house. The first weekend she had dressed up and her father had bellowed at her to go and change into a dress that wasn't halfway up to her backside.

Lily smiled to herself, wondering what the new singer, Davy Jones, would be like. Jo had said everyone was raving about him. They had seen the fabulous Kinks and Gerry and the Pacemakers at Bligh's Hotel. In two weeks, they were going up to London to see Sonny and Cher at the Marquee Club. It was all a dream come true.

They were both cheesed off they had missed seeing The Rolling Stones and The Beatles on stage; they had been too young in1963. Two years later, the two best bands ever were world famous and packed out huge stadiums. The tickets now cost a fortune and they knew it was unlikely that they would ever get to see them. Lily and Jo were nearly sixteen but longing to be seventeen so they could finish school and have the freedom to move to Paris and begin an exciting new life, as far away from their parents as they could easily get.

Half an hour later, the train pulled into the station. Lily jumped out onto the platform, ran up the steps and was relieved to see a Greenline bus waiting outside that would take her to Sevenoaks High Street in five minutes. They were meeting in the Cabana, a coffee shop that was cool and gloomy inside and had the best coffee and cakes in town.

Pushing in through the heavy door, she was enveloped in a cacophony of excited voices. Seeing Jo, she waved.

'Hello, Lily, do you want coffee or shall we get going?'

'Hi, Jo,' she breathed, leaning forward and giving her a hug. 'I'm too excited to eat. Can we go down to Woolworths? I want to buy some new false eyelashes, remember how I lost one?'

Laughing as they remembered that night, they walked out of the gloom into the bright sunshine, Jo hooking her arm through Lily's.

As they perused the make-up and trinkets in the shop, they chatted as if they hadn't seen each other for a week instead of yesterday at school. Then finding what they wanted, they happily ambled out of the Woolworths store and stood admiring their purchases on the narrow pavement. They were oblivious to the people milling around them trying to get past, their focus being solely on Lily's black false eyelashes and Jo's black plastic hoop earrings that had cost them less than a shilling each.

Although Lily lived for summer and hated the grey autumn and dark winters, she felt uncomfortably hot standing there with the sun beating down on them. She was about to say she wanted some shade when Jo blurted, 'Lily, I think I may be in love with a boy called Tom!'

Lily's mouth fell open. Looking at Jo, Lily could see she was uncomfortable with this strange admission. They talked all the time at school and Jo had never mentioned anyone named Tom before. Jo liked boys the way boys liked girls, for sex and fun, but not for the mushy stuff. Before they became such good friends and Lily started staying at Jo's house on Saturday nights, she would come into school on Monday mornings and regale Lily with her exploits over the weekend. Lily was now used to it and was no longer shocked. She admired how gutsy Jo was. Lily was the romantic one, expecting that someday her one true love would come rushing up to her on a big white horse, declaring his undying love! It didn't seem conceivable that Jo had fallen in love, let alone owned up to it.

'I'd like you to meet him at Bligh's tonight and tell me what you think,' said Jo.

'Yeah, okay,' was all Lily could muster, stunned by this revelation. She felt suddenly deflated, wondering if this would affect their friendship and their plans for the future.

'Come on then, don't stand there gawping. Let's get the bus home and start getting ready. It's nearly five o'clock.'

In typical Jo fashion, she set off down the street and Lily had to run to catch up with her. The lazy afternoon was over and they were now a few steps from the bus station. Lily wanted to ask her a myriad of questions but decided to wait until they were on the bus. The Greenline number 22 to Stonebridge was waiting with its engine running. As if they had their own chauffeur, it took off as soon as they jumped on and sat down. Jo eagerly opened a Dorothy Perkins bag and fished out a black linen shift dress that she had bought that afternoon. Lily admired the dress but couldn't contain her curiosity a moment longer. 'Tell me about Tom. Who is he? What's different about him?'

Jo looked up, her brown eyes dancing with amusement or excitement, Lily couldn't tell. 'I've known him for a few months. He's funny, sexy and has gorgeous blue eyes. We've had sex a couple of times and it's amazing. I can't really explain it but I just can't stop thinking about him.'

Lily knew he'd have to be really special for Jo to feel this way. 'Does he feel the same way about you?'

Jo snorted. 'I doubt it, but I'm working on him.'

While the noisy bus wound its way along the country roads, thoughts crowded into Lily's mind. Their friends at school thought it was funny that Lily was the only virgin among them and often laughed about it. Lily thought it even funnier that all they ever dreamed of was getting married and having babies. Lily couldn't think of anything worse. She patiently explained to them, as if they were dim-witted, that she would wait another three months until she was sixteen and could get the new birth control pill from a doctor. She wasn't going to risk getting tied down by becoming pregnant. She told them of her plan to escape her violent father and loveless home and start a new life in Paris with Jo. How they would get good jobs, master the French language and enjoy the passionate culture. She would get married at thirty-two and have a baby at thirty-four. She knew exactly what she wanted.

Sue and Patsy had looked at her as if she was mad. She may as well have told them that they were going to Mars to live with Martians. It didn't matter. Lily and Jo wanted adventure. Neither of them felt the least bit maternal. They would leave as soon as they had finished their 'A' levels and live an amazing life.

Jo's voice interrupted her reverie. 'He doesn't seem to go out with girls, just have sex with them. The love-'em-and-leave-'em type.'

Lily thought this didn't bode too well for a future romance but didn't say.

In no time, the bus was letting them off in Jo's village. They walked as fast as the heat would allow, past the small row of shops and up the hill to Jo's house. Dragging their heels a bit, they were relieved to get through the back door into the coolness of the old brick house. Jo shouted hello to her mum and dad as they went past the lounge room and ran up the stairs to get ready. 'We'll take turns in the bathroom, Lily. You go first while I get my dress out and hang it up. Okay?'

'Okay.' Lily delved into her small overnight bag to get her face washer and toothbrush, glad to have a wash down. Refreshed and back in Jo's room, she took out her dress. It was cool cotton. The front was four large, alternating black-and-white squares, the back was plain black. Next minute Jo was out of the bathroom and bustling her into Jo's mother's bedroom, saying, 'We need a full-length mirror; come on, we'll finish getting ready in here.'

Lily scooped up the transistor radio, along with her things, so they could still listen to their favourite songs blasting out across the North Sea from the Pirate Ship, Radio Caroline. All day and all through the night, they played all the latest bands that had been leaping into the charts since she'd became a teenager in 1963. Goodbye to the crooning voice of Val Doonican and the heart-throb of the late fifties, Engelbert Humperdinck, even to Chubby Checker who had brought them the sensation of 'The Twist'. Hello to The Beatles, The Rolling Stones, The Yardbirds, The Animals, Bob Dylan, The Doors, The Supremes, The Ronettes and dozens more. Lily loved them all with a passion.

Soon they were happily singing along to 'You Really Got Me' with the Kinks and jostling each other for space in front of the wardrobe mirror. They began elbowing each other out of the way and then fell about laughing on the bed. Lying there for a moment to catch her breath, Jo's eyebrows shot up as her glance settled upon the clock on the cluttered dressing table. She jumped up. 'It's ten to seven already! If we get a move on we can catch the ten past bus.'

Smoothing down her mane of natural strawberry blonde hair and taking a last look in the mirror, Jo grabbed her bag off the pink candlewick bedspread and was out the door.

'Hang on, Jo! I can't hurry in these shoes,' yelled Lily, surprised by the sudden rush and wriggling her squashed toes in her white stilettos. Shrugging her shoulders and feeling a bit put out, she looked in the mirror again, checking that her false eyelashes looked okay, slung her bag over her shoulder and followed Jo as fast as she could manage down the wooden stairs. Jo, by this time, had slowed down, complaining that her dress was too short and was riding up even shorter with each step. They ducked their heads around the living room door to say 'goodbye' to Jo's parents.

Mrs Price was sitting on the edge of her armchair, watching the evening news and looking pale and doleful as usual. Mr P, a small, stocky man with balding dark hair, looked up over his glasses and with a mischievous smile said, 'Make sure you're home before the milkman gets here, you two.'

Lily knew he was joking as Jo's dad had a dry sense of humour, but even so, to joke about what time they would come home amazed her. She couldn't conceive, by any stretch of her imagination, her father even making a joke, let alone about the time she should come home on a Saturday night. A picture popped into her head of them getting in around four, just scraping in before the milkman came in his electric cart around dawn. She giggled. Jo looked at her quizzically, then replied,

'Okay, Pops, toodle pip!' She turned and opened the front door and laughing, they scuttled down the narrow path, through the creaky iron gate and down the hill to the bus stop.

The bus arrived just as they got there and they looked at each other and smiled at their good luck. Holding on to the metal rail to steady themselves, they clambered up the steep, winding steps to the top deck. The bus was nearly full. Seeing there was no room in the back seat, they sat near the front, too happy to care, and talked all the way into Sevenoaks.

As the bus shuddered to a halt in the bus depot, they looked at each other in anticipation. Jo because 'he' would be there and Lily because it was breathtakingly exciting to be out of her parents' house and to be able to dress up and actually go out and see a live band. She couldn't wait to get there. They clumped down the steps, trying not to trip and embarrass themselves in their new high heels and shorter-than-normal dresses. They looked striking—Lily in her black-and-white dress and white stiletto shoes, Jo in her black dress, that was at least six inches above her knees and showed an expanse of summer-kissed legs, her feet in shiny black patent sandals. They burst out into the sultry evening air, laughing as they got caught in the tide of people flowing across the street and into the big, old pub.

The first time Lily went to Bligh's Hotel she'd felt like a country bumpkin. The pub was on a corner of the High Street and was a large, impressive building, even more so inside, with its etched glass double doors and cavernous ballroom complete with mirror ball hanging from the centre of the high ceiling. The carpets were the colour of deep emerald and sumptuous.

The dance hall enveloped them as they entered, mysteriously dark, already packed and pulsating with energy. Lily stood still and waited for her eyes to adjust from the bright light outside. 'Hey, Jo, wait, I can't see a thing!' She saw with dismay that Jo couldn't hear her; the band was playing and she was still pushing her way through the crowd. She's probably eager to find Tom, thought Lily, as she tried to keep sight of Jo's back. Jo paused in the midst of the crowd and Lily managed to reach forward and tap her on the shoulder. 'Jo! Slow down. I nearly lost you.'

Jo looked back, her shiny hair swinging. 'Sorry, Lily, I thought you were right behind me.'

They were nearly at the front and stood looking up at the stage in happy silence, letting the music and the energy flow through them. Lily attempted to say something but her words were lost. She let herself drift, as if she were the only one there on an island of sound. The singer had an unusual yet sexy voice. He looked young, maybe eighteen, was skinny and wearing tight blue jeans and a white T-shirt. Feeling someone pulling on her arm, she was reluctantly dragged back to reality. Jo was looking up at her and saying, 'Lily, meet Tom!'

Seeing a stocky, blond, blue-eyed boy staring at her, Lily couldn't help thinking that he wasn't at all what she thought Jo would go for. She had imagined him to be tall, dark and mean-looking. Lily admired Jo for being a confident, complex person, extremely intelligent with a no-nonsense personality. She was around five feet five, two inches shorter than Lily, with an athletic build, an open face and brown eyes that often twinkled with her wicked sense of humour. She had never seemed a sentimental type. Lily was in awe of her. They were so different. Lily often felt painfully shy and was mortified that her breasts had become enormous, seemingly over-night. As they stood together and tried to talk over the music, she began to feel uncomfortable. Tom was looking her up and down. She quickly thought of an excuse to leave them alone. 'Nice to meet you, Tom!' Then turning to Jo, said, 'I'm off to get a drink. See you later.'

They looked surprised but Lily was off across the darkened hall, swallowed up in the crowd like magic. She slowed down as she saw the light coming from the bar. Feeling very conspicuous under the bright lights, she tried to look nonchalant as she walked across the large expanse of green carpet to the counter and ordered a gin and tonic.

'Can I buy you that?'

Her eyes widened in surprise: right in front of her, leaning on the bar, was the singer. She hadn't noticed they'd stopped playing. Lily gave him the quick two-sec-ond-up-and-down look and decided he was definitely not her type. He was about five feet eight with a small frame, pale skin and light brown hair that came down to his shoulders. Lily felt flattered but quickly said, 'Oh, no, thanks. I need to be alone just now.'

He smiled, showing small, uneven white teeth. He looked better when he smiled. His eyes crinkled and for a moment, she felt drawn into them. Strangely, by a trick of the light, one eye looked blue and the other brown. As she wandered away, thinking that he definitely had something, she saw Tom walking towards her.

'Can I buy you a drink?'

'I've just bought one, thanks,' Lily said, holding up her drink to eye level.

He grinned, taking no offence from her hint of sarcasm. 'So where do you come from then? How do you know Jo?'

'I live about twenty miles away in Highden. We go to school together in Tonbridge and I stay at her place sometimes 'cos it's too far to get to my home at night. Are you going out together?'

'Nah, we just see each other around sometimes.'

Poor Jo, he doesn't seem very interested, Lily thought, feeling sorry for her friend. Suddenly live music was coming from the hall again. She brightened and scarpered into it, shouting over her shoulder, ''Bye, Tom,' and disappeared into the dark sea of lively people. She tried to make out faces as she moved through the crowd. She could hear 'Come and talk to me, luv!' and 'Over 'ere, darlin'' but didn't see anyone she recognised. She wanted to find Jo so they could have their usual easy banter or their companionable silence. When she found her, she thought it best not to mention Tom. Jo straight away said, 'What do you think?'

'Yeah, he seems quite nice. I like his cockney accent,' she answered cagily, thinking that he really seemed like a girl chaser and he was short and stocky with freckles. She was relieved when the conversation drifted towards how good the band was and how Jo thought the singer was gorgeous. Lily raised her eyebrows but said nothing. She looked at him again and could see that on stage he did exude a curious magnetism.

Jo told her that she had bumped into her cousin Kate and Tom's brother Carl. Lily always felt wary of Kate, as she was the spitting image of Jo's mother: pale-faced, and her large, round eyes gave Lily the same cold, suspicious look. Nevertheless, she was interested to hear all the goss' that Jo had gleaned. They were soon laughing and relaxed and Lily started to have fun.

It seemed in no time the band stopped for another break and Tom came up to them again. He started talking to Jo. Lily hoped they wouldn't notice if she disappeared to the bar. She turned and prepared to weave her way across the crowded floor but there was a slipstream of people heading that way so she went with the flow. After the anonymity of the blackness in the dance hall, the bar was so bright she felt as if spotlights were shining on her. Everyone seemed to be in groups. She wondered if the two Daves were there. She thought she'd like to bump into someone that she knew as she was beginning to feel like a third wheel. She bought another gin and tonic and glanced around for somewhere to sit and rest her sore feet, just as Tom appeared beside her again. Wishing he'd taken her previous hint, she managed a smile as he was grinning from ear to ear.

'It seems I can always find you at the bar.'

Thinking quickly to hide her embarrassment, she retorted, 'I just thought I'd give you and Jo a chance to talk. You know, three's a crowd and all that.'

'I told you we just know each other, that's all.'

'Right. I hear your brother's here. Did you come together?'

'Nah, we just end up at the same places sometimes. Do you have brothers and sisters?'

'Two brothers but the eldest is twenty and the youngest is ten so we don't have much in common. What about you?'

'Only Carl now, he's eighteen months younger than me. We had a younger brother, Brian, but he drowned in a lake six years ago. I have a half-sister due to my dad buggering off and leaving me mum for her sister.'

'My God! That's awful.' Lily felt she wanted to shrink and disappear. Why had she asked him anything personal?

Tom looked wistful and the light went out of his eyes for a second. 'That's life and ya' just have to get on with it, don't ya?' He smiled again and she was relieved that he'd put things back on a lighter note.

'I have to go back in now and find Jo. 'Bye, Tom,' she said.

Except Jo was nowhere to be seen. 'Sod it!' She realised Jo must have come looking for her in the bar and saw Tom talking to her and stomped off home. Lily started to feel anxious. She began weaving purposely through the crowd, getting her sore toes trodden on and hoping to see Jo chatting to someone, but there was no sign of her. She looked in each of the Ladies' loos, even called her name. Girls looked at her but no one answered. Back in the dance hall, she heard Davy Jones announce this would be their last song. She realised, without a doubt, Jo had buggered off and left her there. Frantically, she circled the dance floor again. Her misery increased as she heard the singer shout, 'Goodnight!'

Everyone whistled and stamped their feet on the wooden floor, making a loud, echoing din. The lights came on and as people started herding towards the door, Lily scanned their faces for Jo. She didn't see anyone she knew and it was a long way home. She perked up as she glimpsed Kate draped around some boy and almost out the pub door.

'Kate, Kate! Have you seen Jo? I can't find her.'

Kate paused, mid-slouch, and half turned to look at Lily. 'Nope, haven't seen her for ages. She's probably gone off with someone to a club.'

'If you see her can you tell her I'm looking for her?'

Kate looked at her as if this would be a huge inconvenience but Lily thought she saw an almost imperceptible nod before Kate turned and went out the door.

Feeling this was a disaster, she wondered how she was going to get to Jo's house. She tried to remember what number was on the bus and whether it said Stonebridge on the front or something else, and did the buses still go after midnight? She hadn't been to Jo's for a month and only three times before that. Wondering if they would have locked her out, Lily tried to suppress her panic. She knew she couldn't get to her own home; it was twenty miles away and the last train would have gone. She gave a mirthless smirk at herself for the folly of her thoughts. As if she could go home in the middle of the night and say she'd lost her friend. Her father would fly into a rage and she wouldn't be allowed to stay at Jo's house overnight ever again. She grimaced. She'd been grounded for a month the last time she stayed at Jo's.

Tom was coming towards her, smiling. She felt relieved. At least his was a familiar face.

'Have you seen Jo?'

'Not for a while. Why, don't you know where she is?'

'No, and I'm staying at her place and I don't know how to get there.'

'I'll take you.'

Two

Lily scrutinised his face to see what his motive was. His blue eyes looked concerned at her distress and he seemed friendly.

'Okay, if you don't mind.' She decided to risk it; besides, what choices did she have?

'We can walk up there. It's not far. It'll only take about half an hour.'

They walked out of Bligh's, past groups of rowdy youths and into the High Street that was now becoming familiar to Lily. The shops still looked inviting even though it was nearly midnight. She could see the pretty summer dresses in the lit window of Richards and then the tantalising array of shoes in Dolcis. On the narrow pavement, their skins touched. She snatched her arm away as if she'd been scalded.

Gradually the shops disappeared and there were just rows of little houses, most with their lights out. There was a bright, full moon lighting their way in the darkness and it was still surprisingly warm.

'Where do you think Jo went?' He seemed relaxed and only mildly curious.

'I think she's gone home.'

'But why would she do that and leave you on your own? Did you have a row or something?'

If only you knew, she thought, but kept quiet.

'I bet she's met some bloke and gone off wiv 'im.'

It was as if Tom was trying to solve the mystery to make her feel better but Lily knew in her gut that Jo had got angry and gone home.

Tom startled her out of her thoughts by stopping and picking a big yellow rose that was hanging over a garden wall. Turning and looking into her eyes, he presented it to her. To hide her surprise, she quickly buried her nose into it, avoiding his gaze. Flowers were one of her greatest loves. The heady fragrance relaxed her. 'Thank you.'

She kept walking and just as they were about to walk over a narrow humpback bridge, Tom said,

'Let's sit on this wall and have a rest.'

Lily's feet were burning with untold blisters so she said, 'Okay,' and plonked herself down on the grey stone wall. She could see the reflection of the moonlight shining on the shallow water as it rushed over the flat stones on the riverbed. Looking up to comment, she found Tom standing so close to her that she gulped. He looked into her eyes saying, 'I think we're going to be together for a very long time.'

Alarmed, she thought that what he was saying was crazy and made no sense. He kissed her before she had time for another thought. His lips were warm and gentle and he had that masculine smell that some boys have. She found it was not unpleasant. She looked into his eyes and could see in the moonlight that they were a clear blue, rimmed with long, blond eyelashes. He was pale-skinned but had a light summer tan over his freckles.

Her memory stirred as she realised he was similar to her first love. Andy was also blond with blue eyes and not very tall. She had met him when she was working on a farm, picking green beans to earn money in the school holidays. It was the summer of '63 and it was hot in the field with nothing to shelter them. They went up and down the rows picking the beans and filling the hessian sacks that they dragged behind them. She had gone to sit on the cool, green grass under a tree for some shade in the tea break. A blond-haired boy with a nice friendly smile and clear, blue eyes had come over to talk to her. She could hear his mates whistling and making fun of him in the background. Undeterred, he introduced himself as Andy, from Waterford.

She found she looked forward to seeing him. Soon they were all bringing their bathers so they could jump gleefully into the brown, swirling water of the nearby river at the end of each sweltering afternoon. The water was cool and refreshing, the bank was slippery mud. Sometimes while they were laughing and splashing around she had seen the occasional fat water rat with coarse brown fur slide off the bank into the muddy water but she had been having too much fun to care. Even the thin, black water snakes weaving their long bodies through the cloudy river didn't faze her. Each time they swam, Andy had to painstakingly remove a calliper from his right leg. Polio had withered his leg as a child and he always had to wear the calliper with a black, built-up shoe. He didn't seem embarrassed. To see him having fun in the water made up for any qualms she felt and she had thought that she was lucky after all.

He asked her out. She remembered walking down Oakhill with him one day. A young couple were sitting on a wooden bench and they had a small transistor radio playing 'I Wanna Hold Your Hand'. He smiled and took her hand in his. She'd felt happy and wondered if this was how it felt to be in love. The bubble lasted nearly a year but as she kept getting taller, Andy stayed the same. Lily felt she was towering over him and her breasts and hips had begun to swell. She no longer felt the safety of being a stick-thin tomboy. She felt self-conscious and decided she wouldn't go out with Andy anymore.

She thudded back to the present as she felt Tom's arms holding her tightly and his hot breath on her neck. All her life daydreaming had got her into trouble and it was getting her into trouble now. She pushed Tom away, saying, 'No, Tom, let's get going.'

Sliding off the wall, she smoothed down her dress and started off across the bridge. Very soon Lily recognised where they were, less than five minutes from Jo's house. As they got closer she could see all the lights were out; the moon had gone behind a cloud and it seemed very dark. Opening the gate carefully so that it wouldn't creak, she turned to him and said, 'Thanks for bringing me here, Tom.'

'I'll wait to make sure you get in. When can I see you again?'

She couldn't see his expression in the darkness but hastily said, 'I can't, Tom.'

Slipping through the gate and gently pushing it closed, she ran up the concrete path and around the side of the house to the back door. Her thoughts were already focused on getting into the house and she didn't give another one to Tom. Carefully she turned the doorknob and gave it a little push, exhaling with relief when it opened. It felt weird creeping into someone else's house after midnight. With a sigh, she pulled off her shoes, carrying them as she crept up the creaking wooden stairs. There was no carpet and each creak was so loud in the silence that it sounded like a rifle going off. By the time she got to Jo's bedroom door she was hardly breathing. She pushed the door slowly and stepped inside, waiting for her eyes to adjust to the blackness. Peering across the room she could see that Jo was in her bed. Lily pulled her dress over her head, dropped it on the floor and, as carefully as she could, climbed into bed.

'Where have you been?' Jo growled angrily.

'I had to walk here. You left without me.'

'Did you screw him?'

'Jo, you know I wouldn't do that.' Lily was shocked that Jo would even think it. 'I'm not going to screw anyone.'

After an expectant silence, Lily added, 'He offered to walk me to your place because I couldn't remember how to get here.'

Jo humphed and turned on her side, facing the wall. Lily felt awful. She wondered what else she could have done. Jo shouldn't have left her. They lay in the darkness, feigning sleep, each tortured by their thoughts. Lily felt wretched, thinking, why, out of all the girls around, does Tom have to take a liking to me? I've been friends with Jo for nearly two years and we've never argued over anything.

Her mind drifted to the time when they went out with the two Daves. It was early June, the first time she had stayed at Jo's house. That night, in Bligh's Hotel, they met the friendly Daves in the bar. They were blond, one with short hair and one with long. Both had blue eyes and easy-going natures. It seemed hilarious to Lily that they had the same names but probably everyone commented on it, so she stayed quiet. Dave T was tall and solid with a pleasant face and curly hair. Dave B was willowy with fine features, a slow grin and wavy hair almost to his shoulders. Lily thought he looked like Jesus. They seemed more interested in their motorbikes than girls. They were funny and talkative. They had asked if Lily and Jo wanted to take a spin down to the Hastings beachfront and get some sea air. Jo had quickly agreed. Lily had whispered, asking her what her parents would think if they didn't go home. Jo had laughed and said they wouldn't care. Lily had relaxed then and felt a thrill as she saw their two gleaming black Triumphs, side by side, in the car park.

She smiled to herself. That was a lark, whizzing all the way down to Hastings at midnight. Dave B had carefully put his spare helmet on her head and strapped it under her chin. How exhilarating it was to take off with a roar onto the A21 and down the coast road, feeling the fresh air rushing by them and the warmth of Dave's body through his black leather jacket. Her false eyelashes had flapped furiously every time she ducked her head around his shoulder to see Jo up ahead of them. Later she discovered that the wind had whisked one away. They slowed down as they saw the lights of the town. It was lit up like a Christmas tree. That was how she had felt, like a kid at Christmas.

The boys pulled up to the kerb on the seafront and parked. She'd looked at the big expanse of beach stretching down to the waves that she could hear but could only see the white froth in the inky darkness. Excitedly she had suggested that they all walk down to the sea, and good-naturedly they agreed. As they sauntered down onto the beach Lily, caught up in the fun of it, half ran and half hobbled over the large pebbles to get to the water. It had been an exceptionally warm night so she'd impulsively pulled her dress over her head and ran into the waves. She'd splashed around in the salty water, swimming a bit, floating around, looking up at the clear night sky, spitting out water as waves went over her. She'd called out to them, 'Come on, you lot, come in with me!'

Then, as if watching a movie, she'd seen a policeman, complete with tall 'bobby' hat, walking determinedly over the pebbles to the water's edge. Through the noise of the waves he'd shouted to her that she couldn't swim in her underwear in a public place and would she please get out. He'd called her 'miss' and waited. As she gingerly picked her way over the pebbles, she found herself wondering, not for the first time, why their helmets were that ridiculous shape. She guessed it was to save their heads being bashed in by unsavoury types lurking in shadows in the streets of London.

Feeling awkward, as she stood dripping wet in her black bra and knickers in front of the young policeman, she'd snatched her gingham dress from Jo's hands and wriggled into it. Apparently satisfied by her now decently clothed body, he had tipped his head, saying, 'Goodnight, then, miss.' As he crunched away on the pebbles, his metal buttons and shiny shoe caps had glinted in the moonlight. They had burst out laughing and went to get something to eat before going home.

She was getting sleepy otherwise she would not have allowed her mind to settle on the following horrendous weekend. They'd gone down to Hastings again on the motorbikes with the two Daves. It had been another warm night. It felt easy being with them. They had sat on a wooden bench, looking out to sea and chatting. A policeman approached them. Looking at Jo he'd asked her if she was over sixteen. Jo unbelievably had told him no.

Then he had looked at Lily and had asked, 'And yourself, miss?' She had answered that yes, she was. He had taken Jo by the arm and told her that she would have to accompany him to the police station. Lily felt panicked as he started to take her friend away so when he turned and asked whether she was sure that she was sixteen, Lily had answered that no, she wasn't. She couldn't let Jo go without her. He paused and had told her, 'Okay, miss, you had better come along too then.'

They were taken to the Hastings Police Station and interrogated. The desk sergeant had asked for their names and dates of birth. After seeming to take an eternity to write that down, he had looked them up and down and had asked them if their parents knew they were in Hastings. They had looked at each other and then in unison, they had told him, no. He had then asked them if they had been drinking or taking drugs. Again, they'd told him no. They were told they would be put in a holding cell until their parents were able to come and get them. Lily still couldn't believe Jo had owned up. It was so unlike her.

Now, remembering that night, the fear and misery came back to her again. They were marched down a long corridor to a small cell. The metal barred door was ajar and was pulled open and they'd been ushered in. The heavy door was clanged shut and locked. As the footsteps retreated and a door slammed, they had looked at each other helplessly. Jo had said with a tight smile that at least they were in the same cell and given Lily a brief hug. Pleased by the unaccustomed affection, Lily had given a feeble smile. There was nothing else they could do except sit on the wooden bench and wait. After an interminable silence, Jo had piped up again and had asked Lily what did she think her dad was going to do to her. Lily hadn't dared to think about that.

At one thirty they'd heard a door open and footsteps approaching. Constable Baker, according to her badge, told them in a matter-of-fact voice that their parents had been informed and they were on their way to collect them. Lily had slumped back on the wooden bench, her heart thumping in her chest. She'd felt hot and there had been no air to breathe in the cell. Her mind had clearly pictured how the phone in their hallway would have been giving its loud, incessant ring in the slumbering house until either her eldest brother, Simon, or her mum got out of bed and went down the stairs to answer it. They would have had to shake her father awake to tell him the news. He would have been groggy at first but as what they were saying dawned on him, his large flabby face would have flushed red, his black eyebrows would have knitted together and he'd have thrown back the bed covers and bellowed like an enraged bull. His anger would have given him enough fuel to ready himself for the hour-long drive to Hastings. She'd optimistically thought that with a bit of luck the long drive might have given him time to cool off.

It seemed like a whole lifetime later that they had heard the door at the end of the corridor open again and brisk footsteps got louder as they approached. The mean-faced policewoman informed them that their fathers had arrived to take them home. Jo had taken Lily's hand and squeezed it. It was three a.m. As the cell door was unlocked, Lily had an irrational urge to hold onto the bars and refuse to leave.

Her father was at the desk talking to the sergeant and had looked subdued. She could see he had shaved and put on a good shirt and jacket, good slacks and polished shoes. She'd known he had made the effort because it was the police. Her father's thin lips were clamped on his rollup cigarette and he was puffing furiously.

As they walked to her father's car, Lily had kept a distance between them. She tried to explain that they weren't doing anything wrong, just sitting on a bench talking and looking at the sea. He kept puffing on his rollup and letting the ash, glowing brightly in the dark, drop down onto his shirt. She knew her mother would be angry with him for burning tiny holes down the front of yet another one. It was unnerving but a relief that he'd never said a word.

Once home Lily ran up the stairs ahead of him and had told him that she was sorry, again. She'd dived into her room, shut the door and made sure she stayed out of his way the next day, but her father had grounded her for a long and miserable month. Tonight was the first night out at Jo's since then. Tears slid down her cheeks. She willed herself to think of a nice memory again but at last, she slipped into a deep, exhausted sleep.

Three

Next morning Lily was very glad to find Jo was her usual self. Luckily, she wasn't the type to hold a grudge. They chatted about the band. Lily volunteered, 'The singer was in the bar when I went in for a G & T and he asked if he could buy it for me.' Seeing Jo's face, Lily trailed off lamely.

'What? Did you have a drink with him?' Jo was looking at her with renewed interest.

'Well, no, I didn't. I s' pose I should have.'

'He was gorgeous! You need your head seeing to.'

Lily shrugged and felt silly but he really hadn't appealed to her. Besides, she had other things to deal with. But she couldn't tell Jo that. They talked about some of Jo's friends but neither mentioned Tom.

After going down to the big kitchen for the traditional fry-up of eggs and bacon, courtesy of Mrs P, Lily was glad to get back upstairs again and collect her things. Jo's mother had never seemed to like Lily, always eyeing her with suspicion as if Lily was leading her daughter astray. Ha to that! But she seemed to accept that they were good friends and would feed Lily when she was there.

Jo's dad was nice. He was fun and interesting in a cranky sort of way. He often had a twinkle of humour in his eyes when he was talking. He took an interest in everything and Lily appreciated his sharp and intelligent mind. She often wished her own father was more like Mr P. They were both keen gardeners but Jo's dad was an avid reader and read books on varied subjects whereas Lily had never seen her father read a book unless the topic was gardening. Mr P would engage them in discussions about politics or what was happening elsewhere in the world. Lily's father would only have conversations when he was out of the house, pretending to be jovial and acting as if he was normal when in company.

Today, Mr P was already out in a chair in the garden, reading the paper. As usual, Jo's elder sister and little brother were nowhere to be seen. Brenda always looked down her nose at them as if they were annoying brats and Paul gave them a wide berth, probably because they were girls.

Lily made sure she thanked Jo's mum for the breakfast. Jo's mum eyeballed her but said, 'That's all right, Lily.'

She'd been looking from one to the other since they came down and Lily guessed she could tell something was amiss between them. They went outside to say goodbye to Mr P. He looked up from his paper. 'It's nice to see you again, Lily, I hope you behaved yourselves this time.'

He seemed to be suppressing a grin so Lily guessed he was joking again and wasn't still cross about having to go to Hastings in the middle of the night.

They wandered down to the bus stop. It was a glorious summer's day and it felt good to be alive. Lily felt a fleeting feeling of happiness as she took in the smells and sounds of summer: the fat, furry bees buzzing by and busily collecting pollen from the fragrant summer flowers; the dragonflies zooming around like tiny iridescent helicopters; birds chirping and flitting from bush to bush. As they walked along, she noticed huge blackberries begging to be picked and eaten on rambling bushes in the ditches. She dived in and picked a couple, putting one into her mouth and giving the other to Jo. The sweet juice burst onto her tongue. Jo smiled at her.

'What? Do I have black around my mouth?'

Jo giggled. Lily rubbed her mouth in case.

The bus arrived at the stop with its noisy engine and smelly diesel fumes. They climbed in and chose their seats, both now quiet and lost in their own thoughts. In no time they were in Sevenoaks and wandering down the cobblestone lane to the Cabana. It was a favourite haunt of uni students in blue jeans and black turtlenecks and anyone who loved a good atmosphere. They talked for a while but there was an uneasy air of unsaid thoughts between them.

'I'd better get the train home, Jo.'

'Okay, Lily. Let's go!' Jo was up and out of her chair. Lily looked up, startled, but noted how slim and taut Jo looked in her blue-and-white striped T-shirt and her denim capri pants. Looking down at her own waistline, she shrugged and joined her at the counter to pay for their coffees and chocolate cake. They walked amicably down Tubbs Hill to the station and onto the deserted platform. As the train pulled out, Lily searched her friend's face and wondered if everything really was okay.

❄

Monday morning came around too quickly and Lily dragged herself out of bed and got ready for school. She yanked on her big navy blue cotton bloomers, struggled with the enormous white cotton bra, pulled the navy-blue-and-maroon checked cotton dress over her head, and thrust her feet into the white ankle socks and black lace-up shoes. Then down the landing and into the bathroom to clean her teeth, wash her face and brush her hair; back into her room to gather up her bag, blazer and straw boater and then down the stairs. Over the banister, she could see her mother standing at the large wooden table in the middle of the kitchen, making sandwiches for her father to take to work. As Lily burst through the kitchen door, Mrs Davis looked over at her daughter, unfazed and accustomed to these dramatic entrances into the kitchen every morning.

'Shall I make your toast, Lily?'

Lily was about to say she didn't want it so thick but her mother had already deftly sliced the loaf into huge doorsteps. The village baker baked the bread in the early hours and delivered it to each customer before six, the problem for Lily being that it was still warm and smelled delicious. It was very hard to resist but Lily knew she now had to watch what she ate so she didn't keep growing at this alarming rate.

'I'll do the spreading, Mum, then you can finish Dad's sandwiches.'

As she took over spreading the creamy butter onto her bread, using only half the normal amount, she could see from her mother's raised eyebrows that she was surprised at Lily offering to help. She shrugged and added a scrape of Bovril, holding the bread between her teeth as she thumped her boater on her head and crammed her blazer into her bag along with the heavy assortment of books. Hooking her bag over her shoulder, she went out the door, eating as she ran down the back steps, down the long path and up the road to the station. Turning the corner into the station drive, she was relieved to see people still arriving but she pressed on a bit faster.

Twenty minutes later, she was trudging up Pembury Road, the long hill to her school. She was glad to see Jo, albeit apprehensive, but smiled when she saw that Jo was pleased to see her. Their classmates chatted animatedly about their weekend but Jo and Lily didn't say much, just stood waiting for the bell to ring.

The day went as usual: assembly in the big hall followed by science in the lab with their teacher who looked like Nana Mouskouri. She had the long, straight, black hair and the black framed glasses, was nice looking in the classical sense and was around the same age as the singer. Her white lab coat came midway to her good-sized calves that had swirls of black hair flattened around them by the neutral-coloured stockings. Lily often expected Miss Andopolous to burst into song with 'I Have a Dream', so strong was the resemblance.

The next lesson was French with the petite, blonde Mademoiselle Champart. She was a joy to listen to as French words flew out of her pouty mouth. Ah! Tre`s bon! Lily knew they were fortunate to have such good teachers and she often scolded herself for her tendency to stare out of the classroom window instead of paying attention.

Before they knew it the bell would ring and they'd move en masse, chatting noisily, down the hallway to the canteen for lunch. The cheery, rotund cooks with their white caps and their flushed cheeks would greet them with, 'What do you want, dearie, the shepherd's pie or the liver and bacon?'

Whatever they chose it would be served up with mashed potato, peas, carrots or sometimes swede or parsnip. Lily did her best to resist the apple pie and custard or the gypsy tart or some other highly fattening thing that they would serve for pudding. The girls always enjoyed their lunch; the cooks seemed to enjoy their jobs and the proof indeed was in the pudding.

As the day wore on Lily longed to hear the last bell. Maths was the last class and not her favourite so as soon as the bell went, she quickly packed her bag and waved to Jo as she went to her bus. Then she took the long walk down the hill to the station. Halfway down, Lily stopped in her tracks. Walking towards her was Tom with his familiar stocky frame and his pale blond hair glinting in the sun. She wanted to turn and run but her bag was too heavy. He broke into a huge smile when he saw her.

'What are you doing here?' asked Lily irritably.

'I wanted to see you.'

'I told you Saturday that Jo's my friend and she's the one that likes you.'

'But it's you that I want to take out.'

That threw her and they walked down the hill in silence for a while. Lily grappled with her thoughts; she was flattered but she didn't want to risk upsetting Jo again.

'I can't stop thinking about you since Saturday and I just had to see you again,' said Tom.

'How did you know I went to school here?'

'You told me.'

'Oh.'

'I got off work early today so I could come and see you.'

Lily felt nervous that Jo's bus would soon be passing by and Jo might see her with Tom. Numerous buses passed, some green, some red double-deckers, and some that were blue and cream with school students crammed into them. Whenever she heard a bus engine she anxiously turned her head and scanned each one. She was aware of most of what Tom was saying but was relieved to see the station and fumbled in her pocket for her season ticket, thinking that once she got past the ticket man, Tom would have to stop and she would escape by running down the steps and onto the platform. But Tom just kept on talking and walked right past the ticket inspector in his navy British Rail uniform and down the steps with her.

Luckily, the train was there waiting for the whistle to blow as soon as the minute hand clicked to twelve on the huge, round station clock, making it four p.m. Hastily Lily opened the carriage door, saying, 'Tom, I've got to go, I don't want to miss my train.' She flung her bag on the seat, snatched her straw boater off her head and slammed the door.

Tom opened it again and asked, 'When can I see you again? Saturday?'

He had a pleading look in his eyes but she was already blurting, 'Jo and I are meeting Susie for her birthday.'

'Sunday then?'

'I work on Sunday at a petrol station, it's a new job.'

'Where?'

'Maidstone.'

The guard's whistle shrilled and the train started to move. Tom pushed the door shut and asked, 'Which one? I'll come and see you.' He looked desperate. The train was gathering speed now and he was jogging along beside it. She didn't know if it was the urgency of the train speeding away or if she was feeling sorry for the boy on the platform but she found herself shouting, 'Greene Street, Shell.'

He had stopped running now. As the train sped away he stood on the platform, gazing after her. She didn't know if he would have heard her reply. She pulled her head in from the window, shrugged her shoulders, sat down and got her books out of her bag. The half-hour journey home was good for getting some homework done and she wanted to stop her thoughts. This is only Monday; Sunday is ages away. He'll never show.

❀

Each day came and went much as the day before. Lily would drag herself out of bed, dress, wash face, clean teeth. Bolt down the stairs, get breakfast. Run to station, trudge up the hill to school. Look for Jo, laugh, talk. Go to classes, have lunch, talk some more. Then, last bell, back down the hill, onto the train. Walk home, get changed and do homework on her bed until she was called for dinner.

This day though, as she lay there, a breeze came through the open window, billowing out the thin pink curtains into the room. It reminded her of when she was about seven and lying on the same black iron bed. Through the open window, she would sometimes hear the sound of girls laughing and a heavy skipping rope rhythmically hitting the ground. Even though she had felt absurdly shy and self-conscious, she wouldn't be able to stop herself going outside and joining in. In no time, she'd be laughing with them as she skipped in and out of the turning rope that they would all take turns holding. During the hot summer nights, darkness would not begin to fall before nine p.m. Then, as if to spoil her moments of fun, her living room window would open and her mother would stick her head out and shout that she had to come in for dinner. She always had to leave right away and hurry indoors, the anxious feeling returning as she went back into the house.

Dragging her mind back to the books in front of her, she tried again to concentrate on the equations. This year was important as it was her O level year. Lily knew she had to work hard to pass as she'd missed a lot through being sick in winter with the usual colds, tonsillitis and bronchitis. Winter was dreary and depressing and she only came truly alive for the three months of summer. She remembered telling Mrs Carroll, her last primary school teacher, that she was going to live in Australia one day where there was endless sun, blue sky and beaches. That's where she would end up, she was sure. On TV, she had seen the Australians laughing as they frolicked in the sea and sunbathed on the sand. The pictures had been in black and white but she had imagined she could see the aquamarine water and feel the warmth of the golden sun on her body. She sighed. It was a struggle doing homework at home and having no-one to discuss the problems with. She was the only one in her village who was at the Girls' Tech. Everyone else was at the high school or the Grammar.

Her mother's voice called up the stairs, 'Lily, come down, your dinner's on the table.'

'I'm coming,' she shouted back as she shoved her books to one side of her bed and went quickly down the stairs. There was still the feeling of anxiety, even though since puberty, her anger towards her father was as strong as the fear. Dinner was something to look forward to as her mother was a great cook but she had to be alert around her father at all times. Her mother, father and two brothers were already seated around the dining table and tucking into their dinner.

'The steak-and-kidney pie looks good, Mum.' That was all she dare say; the TV was on and she didn't want to be shouted at. Her father sat, slowly shovelling food into his mouth, intently watching the evening news as though his life depended on it. He was a huge man, over six feet tall and weighed around eighteen stone. His hands were enormous and so was his head. He had jet black curly hair, big ears and a bulbous nose. His round cheeks and chin that flowed into his large neck always had grey stubble over them by this time of day.

She wished again that they could talk and laugh as a family during dinner as she had seen other families do. This night though, she also wished that someone would ask her how she was doing at school. If only someone would take an interest. As she looked at them, she sensed they were all surviving as best they could in their own way, her mother especially. They sat eating silently around the dining table; those who were facing the TV, her mother and father, would have their eyes fixed on it. Her two brothers would be eating and craning their necks around as much as they could to see what was happening on the screen. Lily usually daydreamed, sometimes wondering what was on TV that night and was there anything that was worth staying down for. A few programs she liked a lot. *Ready Steady Go!* was on Friday nights with Kathy McGowan and was definitely a favourite. She'd seen Donovan with his round, dark-lashed, blue eyes and his dark, soft curls. He had an innocent voice and would sing 'Catch the Wind' and play his guitar and blow on his mouth organ, seemingly all at the same time. Her face softened as she thought of Dave in the Dave Clark Five. He had a flop of dark hair, crinkly brown eyes and was very good-looking. He always had a big grin on his face when he played the drums and sang 'Glad All Over'. She wished that he was her boyfriend, then gave a nervous glance at her father, as if he could read her mind.

It was only Wednesday and none of the good programs were on. *Top of the Pops* wasn't on until Saturday and that was always fun. Jimmy Saville was the compere with his long, thin blond hair, long, thin nose and big, silver rings on his long, thin fingers. He always had the great groups; The Rolling Stones, singing 'Paint It Black' or 'Mother's Little Helper': The Hollies, singing 'Bus Stop' or 'Just One Look'. Maybe Cilla Black or Lulu would be on too. It was a fabulous show and until she started staying at Jo's, it was the highlight of her week. Tonight would be just soaps like *Coronation Street*, a hotbed of personal relationships—awful and compelling at the same time.

Sam, her little brother, suddenly piped up and nearly made her jump out of her skin. 'Lily! Are you going to watch *Doctor Who* tonight? It's on soon.'

'That's good, Sam, I'll watch it with you.'

Simon, Sam and Lily squashed onto the settee and her father took up his place in the big armchair. Their mother started clearing the dinner plates, looking resigned as she took them out to wash in the kitchen sink.

As soon as the program was finished, Lily got up and began to carefully navigate around her father's chair without disturbing him, so she could escape through the lounge room door. As usual, he was assuming the pose of someone sleeping, even softly snoring. His big crumpled face looked deceptively benign and his hands were clasped over his huge belly. When younger she had learned the hard way, rushing by too quickly and knocking his chair. Realising what she had done she had stopped in her tracks, holding her breath. He had snapped into life, enraged by this innocent mistake, and shouted at her, raising his hand like lightning to hit her. Lily, small, skinny and as fast as a rabbit, had run past him and out the door, saying, 'Sorry, Dad.' The fear lay in not knowing what small thing would make him lash out. She felt she was always walking on eggshells and sudden movements still made her involuntarily duck.

Once up the stairs she washed her face, cleaned her teeth, and then hastened down the hallway to the sanctuary of her own room. It was small and narrow, with cream painted walls and pink linoleum on the floor. Her single, black iron bed was against one wall under a window; a white bedside table stood under the other window and a small chest of drawers just fitted in an alcove on the wall opposite her bed. It was hers and she could hide away from her father there; he had never come into her room no matter how angry he was.

She would gladly put on her pyjamas and read for a while. When it was dark, she would then stand on the bed and push the window open as wide as it would go and lean her body out as far as she could to look up at the millions of bright stars; she wanted to check they were still there. It was something constant in her life. The sky was big and expansive. She felt the need to be reminded that there was an unknown world out there, waiting for her to venture into it and become free. As she looked at the stars shining in the darkness, Lily imagined them also shining down on people in Paris or Rome. Even London and that was only fifty miles away. She was mindful that it was the same sky over all of them so nowhere was too far away.

Then she would be glad to lie back down on the bed and drift off to sleep. Often before she fell asleep completely, she would feel she was getting bigger and bigger like the Michelin man. It was a nice feeling. She grew lighter as she expanded so she could float out through the roof into the sky above. It had happened often since she was small and it was comforting. Increasingly, now that she was interested in fashion, before she fell asleep she would see a stunning dress or coat in perfect detail. She knew she had never seen them before and felt sure they were better than anything from the Paris fashions that she'd seen on TV or in the newspapers. The clothes were vivid in her mind. She could see the exquisite colours and the minute detail of the weave of the cloth. Lily would feel happy then and want to go into a deep sleep. She knew she should sit up and draw the stunning designs but she couldn't draw very well and even if she could, then what would she do with them? She wouldn't be able to make them, as she couldn't sew very well either. So she was content to enjoy the beauty of it and drift off to sleep.

Four

Sunday morning came around and Lily's eyes flew open at six thirty. Knowing she had to be at the petrol station by eight o'clock, she jumped straight out of bed. The money was good but she was nervous about doing something new. 'It can't be too hard putting petrol in cars, surely,' she muttered, trying to reassure herself as she got ready. Maidstone was ten miles away and she had to get a bus even though the smell and the vibration of buses made her feel ill. The train, even though by far her favourite, wasn't an option as she would have to change at Paddock Wood and it would take too long. The train was a pretty, relaxing journey as the tracks followed the winding river with green grass and willow trees most of the way. She sighed, knowing the bus would have to do. She put on the cotton slacks and T-shirt that she had put out the night before, did her ablutions in the bathroom and went downstairs. Her mother was already up making a pot of tea. Her father would have to be up soon but she was relieved he wasn't yet. Lily knew her mum would take tea and toast up to him as she seemed to have assumed the role of his servant. Her mum tried to ply her with something to eat but Lily said that she didn't have time and was soon out the back door and down the path shouting, "Bye, Mum.'

Once on the smelly green bus she tried not to think about how it made her feel sick. She chose a seat that wasn't over a wheel arch so there was less vibration that would go through her body and then looked out of the window for distraction. The musty smells of the dark-blue patterned seats and the faint trace of diesel brought back memories of when she was young. Her mother used to take her on the bus to Maidstone every Friday to get the weekly groceries. It was before she was school age and Lily had dreaded it. She'd fight the feeling of nausea until they could get off the bus and then her mother would rush from shop to shop and Lily's little legs had found it hard to keep up. If she was lucky, her mother would suggest they go into Forte's or Littlewoods café for a cup of tea. This would brighten Lily considerably, as that meant she would get a glass of lemonade and maybe a small cake. Her mother didn't talk much to Lily, only to tell her to hurry up or to tell her off.

They would then go back down to the bus stop and her mother's arms would be laden with shopping and she would half push Lily up the steps and half scold her into the bus. The smells would engulf her again and she would often feel sleepy and lay her head on her mother's arm only to be shaken off and told to sit up. Lily felt the despair and loneliness of her childhood and the feeling that there must be something wrong with her for her father and mother to treat her that way. She shook herself to ensure the melancholy fog would not enshroud her; she had to be alert for the day ahead.

Without warning, her thoughts turned to Tom. She wondered if he'd come to see her today. It seemed unlikely he'd go all that way. It was intriguing that he liked her so much but as soon as she entertained any thoughts of him she would think of Jo. She felt sad and wished he had those feelings for Jo instead. How much simpler it would be. It seemed to Lily that the one we take a liking to never seems to be the one who likes us. It always happened like that. She'd liked Roger but he knew it and he seemed to take pleasure in making fun of her in front of his mates. Or there were boys that took a shine to her that she had flat out no interest in.

After half-a-gruelling hour of stopping and starting for passengers and traffic lights, she jumped off the bus, took a gulp of fresh air and made her way through the deserted town to the petrol station. Seeing the 'Shell' sign, she walked across the empty forecourt, then taking a deep breath, she went into the office. Mr and Mrs Hall had their heads together looking at a paper on the counter. They looked like nice people. Mr Hall was short with a solid build; he had dark, wiry hair with a bald spot like a monk in the middle and a lot of hair sprouting out of his ears. Mrs Hall was taller with blonde, permed hair and a buxom, full figure.

'Ah! You must be Lily Davis. Glad to see you're on time, Lily. The wife and I like punctuality, don't we, dear?' They smiled at each other in agreement. 'Right, young lady, let's go out to the pumps and I'll show you what you need to do.' He rubbed his hands together and walked out to the pumps with Lily quickly following him. 'As people draw up in their cars you must ask them what sort of petrol do they want and how many gallons. Then take the petrol cap off and put it on the car roof. You have to be very careful to put it back on, Lily, as many people have driven off with it still on the roof. You must always offer to check the oil and water and wash the windscreen. Each bonnet is different; the latch has to be found by feeling around under it and then releasing it and putting it up on its metal arm. I'll show you on my old Mercedes over there.' He demonstrated and then stepped back. 'Do you want to try that?'

Lily fumbled around feeling for a catch, not knowing what it would feel like, but with grim determination she found something that could be it and managed to click it free. Mr Hall seemed pleased. 'Then take the oil stick out and wipe it on a rag, put it back in and then pull it out again to see where the oil comes up to on the stick. If halfway or less, tell them they need oil. Go over by the shop door and get a can of oil out of the rack, twist the cap off of where the oil goes and put it in.'

Lily felt panic coming on. What if she put the oil in the wrong hole? They all looked quite similar under the bonnet. She thought that she really must concentrate.

'Check the water in the windscreen bottle and fill it with water if necessary. Always make sure caps are screwed back on tightly. Got all that, Lily?'

Mr Hall had kindly eyes and a weather-beaten face. His skin looked blackened as though the years of having his face stuck in engines and under cars had caused the oil to become ingrained. She liked him. 'Yes, Mr Hall.'

'Then add up what it comes to and bring the money into the office and the missus will check it and give you change and a receipt. Any problems ask me or the wife, okay?'

'Okay, Mr Hall.'

He started to hurry off and then stopped and said over his shoulder, 'And remember to smile and be friendly.'

She realised she must be looking worried and serious and made a mental note to relax. She heard an engine and turned to see her first customer coming into the court in a dark green Mini Minor. She took another deep breath, thinking, okay, here goes.

People were mainly nice. Soon she felt she was getting the hang of it. There didn't seem to be any pressure to hurry so she took her time looking for each cap, remembering to screw them back on tightly and doing mental arithmetic to add up the cost.

A loud muffler sound made her turn and see a shiny, fiery-red car with lots of gleaming chrome come swooping in. She guessed it may be American. Lily looked everywhere for the petrol cap. She felt an idiot but in the end she had to bend down to the driver's window to ask, 'Where's the petrol cap?'

The bloke inside seemed too tall for the car. He had a tan, and chiselled features, black hair and small eyes. He smirked and seemed amused that she couldn't find it and told her it was at the back and under the number plate. Right, she thought irritably, he could have bloody well told me that in the first place.

When she took him his change he said, 'Would you like to take a spin in my Mustang when you're finished here?' He was leaning a tanned, well-muscled arm on the wound-down window, looking cool and confident.

'No, I wouldn't. Thanks, anyway.'

He roared off and she was glad she hadn't had many like that. He looked about thirty and was probably married.

Lily found she didn't mind the smell of petrol. It was different to diesel, almost a pleasant smell. It was a busy day and she was getting hot and tired. Around one o'clock they gave her an egg-and-lettuce sandwich and an icy can of Coca Cola and that kept her going for another few hours. She was just thinking it must be nearly four and time to go, when she saw Tom come around the corner, looking tanned and relaxed. She felt surprised and flattered and thought she may have blushed. She didn't acknowledge him and finished with one last customer and hoped her cheeks had drained again. Looking at her Timex she could see it was now five past four and went to see the boss for her pay.

'You did well today, Lily, same time next Sunday?'

'Yeah, thanks, Mr Hall, see you then.' She walked out and looked down at the brown envelope they had given her, pleased to see a one pound and a ten-shilling note in it. She joined Tom on the pavement. 'I didn't think you'd come.'

'I told you I would.' He was smiling from ear to ear and his eyes looked warm and mischievous.

'Shall we get a drink and something to eat at the Wimpy Bar? I'm starving.'

'Yeah, I'd like that.'

They walked up Greene Street and up to the now busy High Street. People seemed to be either scurrying along, probably eager to get home, or sauntering along the pavements looking in shops as if not wanting the day to end. Lily couldn't resist eyeing off all the clothes in the shops until she saw the Wimpy Bar come into view. They went in and it was a hive of activity. Everything smelled good so they had burgers and chips and a coke each and sat down in a red vinyl booth with a grey Formica table.

Lily bit into her burger, avoiding having to look at Tom. She felt at home in Wimpy Bars as she used to work in their Tonbridge branch on Friday evenings. She had fun some of the time but found it didn't suit her nervous disposition, what with the boys eyeing her up and commenting on her legs or breasts. She found the stress outweighed the fun and quit after a couple of months.

Tom looked up from his burger and said, 'I want to take you out, will you come to Bligh's with me next Saturday?' Lily looked down at her plate, not knowing what to say. He obviously really liked her and Jo did say that they weren't actually going out and it seemed he was only interested in the sex. Even so, Jo seemed to have the unspoken hope that it might blossom into love in time.

Her mind raced; what should she do? She could tell he was in love with her. He'd said he'd never felt this way before. Lily felt she'd never been loved by anyone, not her parents or anyone. She was just there, existing. Her next-door neighbours, Fred and Sylvie, showed her more care and concern than anyone else in her life. Their front door was opposite hers and they shared the same path. Many times over the years, if upset or frightened, Lily would run out of her front door and knock on theirs. They always welcomed her with open arms and would say, 'Poor little love, in you come.' Thank God for them in her life.

Jo might love me, she mused; she's never effusive about anything but I know she cares. She became aware that Tom was looking at her curiously; he was probably wondering why she was such a daydreamer. She had to give an answer. She knew that if she didn't soon get the bus home she would get into trouble, so she said, 'Tom, I can't meet you next Saturday as Jo and I are going up to London to see Sonny and Cher. I'll have to see how Jo feels about it but perhaps we could meet the following Saturday?'

Tom beamed his relief. She was glad from his reaction that she'd said yes. 'Now we'd better get going, I have to catch my bus. You can ring me; I'll give you the number.'

They left the cosy hum of the Wimpy Bar and went out into the street. It was still warm and daylight. Lily turned to him and asked, 'Are you coming to the bus stop?'

'I'll walk you there but I'm going to run home, I've spent all me money now.'

'You're kidding? It's got be eight or ten miles?'

'I'll be okay. I'm fit and it's a nice day.'

She never felt sure if he was joking with her. 'Wow! Okay then. I'll write down my number. Put the phone down if Dad answers, which is very unlikely, but if it's Mum, she's all right.'

He had that happy look on his face again. The sun was shining on his pale blond hair. He had a nice wide smile and even, white teeth. His blue eyes said more than his words. He kissed her gently; Lily kept her eyes open as they were in a busy street. It felt nice. She turned away, gave him a wave and stood at the bus stop. But then it suddenly dawned on her that she could have given Tom the money for a bus ticket. She hadn't even thought of it. Feeling terrible, she quickly turned to see if she could call him back but there was no sign of him. Shrugging her shoulders, she carried on waiting.

The Greenline number 44 made a noisy arrival and she clambered on. Looking out of the window as the bus took its winding route out of the town and down Linton Hill, seeing all the pretty-looking pubs scattered along the way brought a smile to Lily's face. The big hanging signs were works of art, depicting the pub name. She saw the 'The Star', 'The Speckled Hen' and 'The Unicorn'. There were wooden tubs of pink-and-purple petunias and bright orange marigolds making striking splashes of colour in their driveways. Wistfully, she wondered how many people were inside, talking and laughing as they shared a joke over a pint or a gin and tonic.

The buildings gradually disappeared and the scenery became green rolling fields, some with horses in them. Strangely, when she was around ten, she found that her father and she had something in common: they both had a love of horses. He had grown up on a farm but Lily had never asked him what it was like or whether he had ridden horses there. Her grandfather was a mean and evil-looking man and she could well imagine that her father was beaten as a child as well. On the Sunday evenings that her grandfather came to play cards, Lily stayed away from him and even hated the smell of him. He always wore the same suit that had a musty odour and his hair was slicked back with Brylcreem that smelled rancid after probably being on his hair for weeks. He had never said anything nice to her and seemed to think he could tell her what to do.

One day some people were riding horses through the village and Lily had begged her father to let her have one. She could tell he really wanted to say yes but he reminded her that they didn't have room for a horse. She told him that he had a huge amount of room up at his allotment where he grew his vegetables. He'd replied that it wasn't his land. He'd sounded exasperated but she'd known it was more that he couldn't let her have a horse, rather than exasperated with her for a change. Knowing it wasn't possible she decided to be brave and go and talk to a pretty girl with brown curly hair that she had often seen riding ponies around a cobblestone yard just outside the village. Shyly she had introduced herself; the girl on the pony smiled and said her name was Ivy. They were a similar age and soon became good friends, riding together at weekends.

It had been a dream come true for Lily. Ivy was from London but came down to see her grandfather who owned a big rambling farmhouse a couple of miles from Lily's home and near her mother's work. He had stables set around a cobbled courtyard and several horses and ponies. He was a small, gruff, eccentric man and looked like a leprechaun. Lily was touched that he allowed her to ride his precious horses. Ivy eventually moved to Highden with her parents but went to Tonbridge Girls' Grammar School. When Lily discovered this she wondered again if this was the choice that she should have made instead of the Girls' Tech. If she'd known Ivy would be there it would have made a difference.

At last the bus pulled into Highden and Lily was glad to get off it and get up the path to her house. She was bone tired and wanted to have a bath and go to bed early. It was nearly dinnertime but she wasn't really hungry. She decided that she wasn't going to tell them that she went to the Wimpy Bar and she would just have a bit of cake. She wondered what cake her mum had made today. Lily hoped it was a Victoria Sandwich, with raspberry jam and fresh cream in the middle. Her mother always made a huge roast for Sunday lunch and a salad and cakes for Sunday tea. She hurried up the path in anticipation but also so as not to attract attention by being late.

Five

Lily found her thoughts often turning to Tom. She knew he was different from any other boy who'd chased her. Other boys had annoyed her by trying to fumble their way into her knickers. She had felt infatuated from time to time but it usually wasn't reciprocated. This suited her melancholy disposition and she'd sing along at the top of her voice to all her records with the heart-wrenching lyrics. Tears would roll down her cheeks and she enjoyed the yearning. She didn't know what she was yearning for. It hadn't been skinny Roger or unsuitable Jeremy but a longing to be close to someone, a special someone that the artists on her records were always singing about. It all seemed so romantic. She wondered if there really is just one perfect person for each of us. If so, she knew she was young and she'd have to wait. She didn't mind really, she just wanted the day to come when she would leave school and start her new life. She didn't need a boyfriend; she had Jo and their soon-to-be-realised goal of leaving dreary England behind them.

Today though, for once she didn't feel like listening to her records. There was no yearning for Tom. They had skipped the part where they knew each other for a while and felt an attraction from afar. There had been no flirting stage with him. No dancing around each other that normally leads to getting to know one another and then maybe some kissing. He'd fallen in love and she'd held her distance.

Feeling hot and restless, she couldn't sleep. Tossing and turning, her mind kept going over and over the dilemma of Tom and Jo. Strangely, as far as she could tell, he seemed to genuinely love her. She thought of him running all the way back to Chitswood from Maidstone and knew he must be keen to do that. The thoughts kept going around in her head until she fell into a fitful sleep.

At daylight her eyes sprang open. She decided to get up early so that she could catch the same train as Ivy. She needed to talk to someone about this dilemma. As she lay there she briefly considered confiding in Sarah next door, Fred and Sylvie's daughter, but at one stage Lily had gone out with a boy called Robbie and Sarah became very keen on him. Lily only saw him a few times but Sarah became secretive about the subject. She found out later that Sarah was now going out with Robbie. Lily hadn't minded but she didn't feel she could open up about Tom to her. Throwing back the covers, she jumped out of bed, got dressed and packed her school bag. There was no-one in the bathroom so it was in and out with a wash of her face and a quick clean of her teeth.

Her mother looked surprised at being interrupted before seven. 'What are you doing up so early?'

She seemed to be having a rare bit of peace, sitting in her kitchen chair, drinking a cup of tea, still in her fluffy, pale-blue dressing gown with matching slippers and her hair net on.

'I want to catch Ivy Thompson today, Mum. She gets an earlier train.'

'In that case, you must have time for some toast today then, it's only just seven.'

'Okay, Mum, just one small slice of the Hovis, thanks.'

'There's tea in the pot, want a cup?'

'Yes, please.'

Mrs Davis looked pleased that Lily was accepting her offer of breakfast and got up and busied herself with slicing the Hovis and pouring the tea out of the pot with its red-and-green-striped knitted tea cosy. Lily kept her eye on the clock and knew she had twenty minutes to spare. It was quite nice sitting quietly with her mum in the kitchen, enjoying her breakfast for a change. At seven fifteen she picked up her school bag and said, ''Bye, Mum, thanks for breakfast.'

She went to rush out the door and run down the steps as usual but remembered she didn't have to this morning. The sky was clear blue and the sun was shining. She was enjoying the summer, and wondered why it couldn't always be as good as this. Taking her time to the station for a change, she thought maybe she should do this more often. She knew she wouldn't though. She almost always felt like pulling the covers up over her head and staying in bed, especially if it was a cold, dark or rainy morning. It was often all three.

Lily always walked at a brisk pace but now she strolled down the long path, turning left at the bottom, past the small sweet shop that still had the enormous, old glass jars filled with an array of coloured sweets in the window. When she was small she'd go into the shop brimming with anticipation and buy four sherbet disks and eight spearmint chews and have to tiptoe to give Mr Jones her few pennies. She quickened her pace and passed the tiny supermarket and the big, old pub. As she rounded the corner she could see the station and had to resist the urge to break into a run as her body seemed programmed to do.

As soon as she was on the platform she could see Ivy waiting at the far end, her brown curls glinting in the early sunshine. She waved as she got closer. 'Hey! Ivy!'

''ello, Lily, surprised to see you 'ere so early.'

'Yeah, I know. I really need some advice and I thought we could sit together and you might be able to help.'

Once they were comfortably ensconced on the train Lily blurted out, 'Ivy, there's this boy called Tom who has fallen in love with me. Trouble is the same day I met him Jo 'fessed up that she's mad about him. We went to Bligh's to see Davy Jones and Jo introduced me to Tom. He kept staring at me and I felt uncomfortable so I kept going off to the bar to get a drink.'

Ivy laughed her deep, throaty laugh; she couldn't help herself. 'Yeah, that'd be right.' Another look at Lily's face and she quickly shut up again.

Lily blabbed the whole story to Ivy, making sure to leave nothing out. Finally saying, 'He's asked me to go to Bligh's with him in a couple of Saturdays' time and I don't know what to do. I'll have to tell Jo today. Do you think I'll lose her as a friend when I tell her?'

'You might, depends how much she wants him, but honestly, Lily, from what you're telling me, I can't see why you're risking it.'

'It's hard to explain, it's just different. He's fallen in love with me. What would you do if you were Jo?'

'I'd scratch your bloody eyes out, friend or no bloody friend.'

Lily could see that for once, Ivy wasn't laughing.

'Have you ever been in love with anyone, Lily?'

'Well, there was Andy. Do you remember him? I was probably too young to love him but he was special. I mainly seem to have strong infatuations. Like Andy's friend, Jack from Goudhurst. He looked like Donovan.'

'Yeah, he was gorgeous. And don't forget Jeremy from the farm, you had it bad for him for a while.'

'Yeah, I know, but that was just a crush too.' Lily sighed as she reflected on her patchy romances, real or imagined. 'Greg was nice. He even took me to visit his house and meet his family a couple of times, but I think it was the same thing: he seemed to love me and he was easy to be with. He didn't pressure me to have sex. The thing with Jo may be all one-sided. They haven't been out on a date.'

They sat in silence for a while, both contemplating the dire situation. The train pulled into Tonbridge station and they piled out with the other commuters. As they walked up the hill Ivy said, 'Look, Lily, I think you're going to have to risk it and tell Jo the truth, like you've told me. See what she says. She may give you an ultimatum and then you're going to have to either choose Tom, who sounds like a wanker to me, or Jo, who you spend a lot of time with.'

Lily digested this advice and decided that was what she'd do. 'Thanks, Ivy. You're a good friend.' She gave her a brief hug.

They were at the Grammar school already so they said their goodbyes and Lily kept going up the hill. There was a feeling of dread about facing Jo. Lily couldn't help thinking how her life could have been so different if she had chosen the Grammar school on that fateful day at primary school. Then she wouldn't have met Jo and she wouldn't have met Tom. Ivy would have probably been her best friend and she would have stuck to riding horses.

Six

Lily dreaded telling Jo that she had been asked out by Tom and that he wanted to meet her at Bligh's the Saturday after Jo and Lily's outing to see Sonny and Cher. She knew she had to; Ivy's words were still repeating in her head and she felt deceitful. Anyway, it had to be faced that Tom had fallen in love with her; she couldn't keep pretending that it wasn't happening.

At lunch Lily toyed with her food. She could see Jo was aware that she was acting strangely so she suggested that they go outside and sit on the grass to get some sunshine. When Lily had something on her mind she wasn't good at keeping it to herself for long.

'All right, good idea, come on then.'

They sauntered down the rabbit run of corridors and then out through the big glass doors to the school grounds. Surveying the packed grass area, they could see that most of the girls had the same idea and were lazing around in the afternoon sunshine. As soon as they found a patch of green grass big enough to stretch out on, Lily blurted it out. 'Jo, Tom came and saw me for a couple of hours at work yesterday. He says he's in love with me and no matter what I say to him, he won't go away.' She looked into Jo's eyes, imploring her to understand.

'Yeah, I know! He's got the hots for you and you're right, there's not much you can do about it.'

Lily stared incredulously at her friend. She never ceased to amaze her. Jo was always down to earth and logical but she didn't think she would be about this. 'So it's okay with you then?'

'Has to be, doesn't it?'

'Thanks, Jo. I've been so worried. I never wanted this to happen. I'm more surprised than you are. You know I'd never want to hurt you, don't you?'

'Yeah, I know. It'll pass and I can wait. Funny thing is, while I've been waiting to see how this was going to play out, I've taken a fancy to his brother, Carl. He's a laugh and easy to be with so we've got together a couple of times.'

Lily didn't know what to say, this was getting stranger by the minute. 'What's he like?'

'He's very different to Tom but in many ways they feel the same. They have the same cockney accent and sense of humour and I enjoy his company. They're both randy and like lots of sex.' Jo laughed and seemed genuinely okay with the situation.

'I'd like to meet him, he sounds nice. Will it be all right if we all meet up at Bligh's the Saturday after this then?'

'Yeah, course. You gonna have sex with him?'

'Jo, you know I'm not going to have sex with anyone 'til I can get on the pill. Just over two months to go now. I wonder how come you get away with it.'

'Dunno! Maybe I'm sterile!' She was still laughing but then her face became serious as she said, 'I want to get a career in science and us to live in Paris like we've planned so it suits me for now. No nappies or doing dishes.'

They laughed together and lay looking up at the blue sky, not saying anything for a while.

'So what happened? How come Tom came all the way over to Maidstone to see you?'

'Well, I didn't like to tell you, but I was halfway down the hill last Monday and I couldn't believe my eyes, there was Tom walking up to meet me.' Lily carefully told the whole story, all the time eyeing Jo to gauge her reaction. When she got to the bit where they went and had Wimpy burgers after she finished work and Tom had run back to Chitswood, Lily trailed off.

Jo's eyes had widened at the unlikely story and she looked at her friend in astonishment. 'Wow! He has got it bad. It must be your big green eyes and those big breasts of yours, Lily.'

'Yeah, right. Is that why all boys fall at my feet and ask me out then?'

Jo had to agree that didn't seem to be generally the case and the look on each other's faces made them burst out laughing. The bell went and they got up and walked companionably into the school. Lily felt so relieved at

Jo's response, she felt like hugging her. She restrained herself, not wanting Jo to feel embarrassed.

As the afternoon wore on, Lily realised she felt happy. The dread of upsetting Jo had lifted from her like an oppressing black cloud and she thought it could be fun, the four of them out together. She found herself daydreaming again and she peered up anxiously at Mr Sanders, her maths teacher, to see if he'd noticed. He was always onto her about her daydreaming, and he'd pulled her up on it a few times in front of the class. It made her feel like a knucklehead. He didn't seem to have noticed so she quickly looked down at the maths book and tried to concentrate on the numbers on the page and the sense she had to make of them.

Seven

Lily was so excited that they were going to London that she sprinted up the hill to the fruit shop on Saturday morning, as if the faster she went the faster the morning would go and she'd soon be on the train to meet Jo. She smiled cheerily at all the customers knowing that in three hours she would be back home and soaking in a bubble bath, then getting her bag to catch the train to meet Jo in Sevenoaks.

Racing home again, she ran the bath and carefully packed her dress and shoes in her bag. She put a copper rinse through her hair and then wallowed in the warm bubbles for the twenty minutes it took for her hair to look red and shiny. Normally she could relax in the bath for ages but today it was impossible to stay still for long. She couldn't remember when she had last felt so happy. All the recent angst about Tom was far from her mind.

The train pulled in to Sevenoaks at three thirty. Jo was in the Cabana talking to Kate when Lily arrived. They looked up as Lily approached; it seemed to Lily, both looking a bit uncomfortable at the sight of her. Instinctively she knew they'd been talking about her. Kate stood up, scraping her chair on the floor. 'Hi, Lily, you can sit here, I'm just leaving.'

Lily sat down warily and when Kate went out the door, asked Jo what Kate had been saying.

'Oh, you know Kate; she's asking about how I'm coping with Tom chasing you. I told her I'm going out with Carl at the moment, which was awkward in itself as Kate had a thing about him for a while. She can be a real bitch though and I'm relieved you're here as her negativity gets to me. I don't want anything to spoil the high I'm on knowing we're going to London tonight to see Sonny and Cher.'

Lily wrestled with the uncomfortable feelings that were now threatening to swamp her. 'So what did she say about me? She's never liked me.'

'The usual crap you'd expect: like how do I feel about it? She refuses to believe you're a virgin and thinks you're having me on. Come on, Lily, let's not waste time on what Kate thinks, let's just have fun.' Jo's face softened, the hardness replaced with childlike eagerness.

Lily couldn't help smiling at the transformation and felt the anxiety melt out of her body. 'I just need to pop into Boots as we go past.'

'Cool, let's do it! I might buy some perfume.'

Lily laughed at the thought of Jo wanting to wear perfume. She was rarely that girly. They ran to Boots, unable to contain their excitement now that the time was here after weeks of planning.

It seemed in no time at all they were walking back down to the bus stop in Stonebridge, made up and dressed in their best gear. They were hoping they looked sophisticated so they could get into the club without scrutiny. Lily was wearing the highest heels she owned, black, shiny patent and strappy. Her dress was short and black with a clear plastic strip around the waist. She wore white plastic earrings and a white bangle and thick false eyelashes that she fancied made her look like a model. Jo was also wearing black, a slinky jumpsuit with a back so low it was almost down to the waist. Jo was lucky that she could get away with no bra. Feeling a bit overdressed for Stonebridge, they caught the seven o'clock train from Sevenoaks up to London.

Lily had been to London a few times but only to look in the shops in Oxford Street, always getting out at Charing Cross station so as not to get lost. She would wander down to the fountains in Trafalgar Square, sit on a wall and watch the tourists and day-trippers feed the hundreds of pigeons. She didn't like pigeons or that they continually shat over everything, including the magnificent bronze lions and Lord Nelson's column, but ignoring that, there was always a fun atmosphere of people enjoying themselves and it would lift her spirits.

She had never been in London at night and even though they got out at Charing Cross station, it looked very different lit up in the night sky. There was singing coming from St. Martin-in-the-Fields. Lily had wandered in there a couple of times, unable to resist the magnificent church with its columns and the subterranean world of its crypts. Tonight, there were crowds of people talking and laughing as they walked along the streets, probably on their way to pubs or restaurants, or maybe a show. It was a world away from Highden.

There were brightly lit red double-decker buses crawling along the busy streets; black taxis were tooting their horns and Lily craned her neck to see what the people inside of them looked like. Jo decided they would walk up to Wardour Street and enjoy the scenery along the way. Lily drank in all the sights as they sauntered along, past Piccadilly Circus with its flashing neon signs advertising Coca Cola and such like. It looked like the flashy pictures she'd seen of Las Vegas. She was fascinated by the statue of Eros in the middle of the frantically busy roundabout. She wondered who on earth would have thought it was a good idea to put the god of love in such a noisy place and knew he must hate it there.

They asked a group of young, cool-looking guys for directions and were told to follow them, which turned out a bonus as they were admitted into the club without any scrutiny as they trailed in behind them. The Marquee Club was like a big party. Cher's voice was deep and sultry as they sang 'I Got You Babe' side by side, looking into each other's eyes, hers dark brown and Sonny's blue. They seemed completely in love and in tune with each other. Cher was very tall with lustrous, straight black hair cascading down almost to her waist. Her faded blue jeans made her legs look incredibly long. The pale fur sleeveless jacket over the soft white shirt gave a careless look of chic glamour. She looked like a gypsy but Lily had read somewhere that she was part Cherokee Indian. Sonny's light brown hair came almost to his shoulders. His eyes crinkled all the time as he was always smiling. He wore a white shirt and jeans too. He never took his eyes off Cher. Nobody did.

Lily, even in her wildest dreams, had never imagined herself in a London nightclub. All the boys were good-looking and smartly dressed. They mostly wore dark suits and white or pink shirts with the Beatle-style collar with gold pins through them. They wore skinny black ties. One boy with dark hair and smiling eyes came up to her and opened his hand. She looked down and saw three red pills that looked like Smarties. She smiled and shook her head. She was on such a high she didn't need drugs. It was the best night of her life.

❁

The following Saturday was the day of her date with Tom. Getting ready for her job, Lily had mixed feelings about the upcoming evening. She mused that they would just have a few drinks and listen to the band then it would be time to catch the train back home again for work the next day. She decided it would all be okay.

Gathering up her bag, she rushed out the door and was soon hurrying up the steep hill, past the church and into the village. It was the first shop and she slipped in just on time. She smiled at Mr and Mrs Bates and they acknowledged her with quick smiles as they were already serving customers. Lily knew the keen shoppers would have been queuing outside at eight thirty, eager to get on with their day of watching cricket on the village green with a picnic rug and a picnic basket or meeting up with friends for a drink at lunchtime. She put her bag out the back and put on an apron and began serving.

Mr Bates was tall and thin, in his sixties and a cockney. He loved to make jokes with the customers. If someone was looking into a bin of potatoes and asked, 'Are these King Edwards?' his quick reply would be, 'No, madam, they're yours once you've paid for them!'

Everyone would laugh, including Lily who had heard him say it many times. They all enjoyed the Vaudeville antics and she often felt like joining in and saying, boom, boom, but she would feel too shy.

As she was bringing out punnets of luscious, sweet-smelling strawberries to put on display, Mrs Bates said, 'Lily, you can go now, it's twelve o'clock.' She followed Lily out the back and pressed a ten-shilling note into her hand.

'Thanks, Mrs Bates. I'll see you next week.'

Lily rushed back down the hill again and caught the train to Maidstone to buy something to wear that evening. Martins was her favourite shop, she bought all her clothes there. It was cheap but the designs were brilliant. She admired the black-and-white dog-tooth-check jacket with a matching mini-skirt. The staff had teamed it with a white blouse with a frill down the middle but it was too dressy for her. She liked the geometrical shift dresses. One with bold orange and pink alternate squares back and front caught her eye but she already had one in black and white so decided on a striking red shift. She tried it on and thought its straight lines made her look slimmer. It was only about three inches above her knees so her father couldn't complain. Some girls were wearing them about twelve inches above the knee. Admittedly, this was in London rather than down in Kent in the 'sticks' but she wished she could be more daring. The price was eight shillings and ninety-nine pence. She handed over her ten-shilling note gladly, then without lingering she went straight to the station so she had time to get ready for her night out.

It was four o'clock by the time she got home. The house was quiet. Thinking they were probably asleep in front of the TV, she ran upstairs, glad to have no-one bothering her. After putting the dress on a hanger and smoothing out the creases, Lily ran herself a bubble bath and allowed herself to relax in the warm scented water, washed and dried her hair, and brushed it until it shone. Then, dressing nicely but not too nice so her father would notice and question her, she reluctantly left off her false eyelashes. She was wearing her white leather boots that had small square cut-outs at the top, just above her ankles. She hoped they wouldn't be too hot. They had small kitten heels, and were comfortable and suited her as she was already five foot seven inches tall. She didn't want to go into the lounge and risk being interrogated so she put her head around the door and saw that they were watching *Bonanza* on TV.

'I'll be back on the ten o'clock train as I'm going to work tomorrow. 'Bye, Mum! 'Bye, Dad!'

They roused a bit in their chairs but didn't turn to look at her. ''Bye then, duck,' her dad said gruffly. They were used to her staying at Jo's house now.

She got to the station with a few minutes to spare. The train was nearly empty, and wasting no time, she went into the tiny toilet cubicle to put some mascara and eyeliner on. She liked the black-eyed look. Her hair was in a Mary Quant style, short at the back and long at the sides with a fringe straight across. It was normally light brown in colour but the copper-coloured rinse that she'd been putting through brought life to it. She backcombed the top a little to get some height and then put in white plastic-hoop earrings. As she bent forward to peer into the tiny mirror, the overpowering toilet smell repulsed her and she had to get out. She went looking for somewhere to sit. A group of boys couldn't resist whistling and making comments. She felt she'd never get used to it. There had been a bonus to having been skinny and invisible before she became a teenager. She moved as far away as she could, down to the other end of the carriage.

As the train pulled into Tonbridge station, she noted how the station was deserted compared to eight on a

Monday morning. There were a few very smartly dressed people on the platform who were probably going up to London to see a show, 'up to town' as they would have put it. A feeling of relief flooded through her knowing she was free for a while from school and home.

Fifteen minutes later the train pulled into Sevenoaks. The station was a fair hike from the town and up a big hill. She could either stride up the hill or catch a smelly bus. The bus was waiting so she jumped on and ran up the stairs to the top deck. Lily had arranged to meet Tom at the Cabana. She liked going there as the smell of roasting coffee met her nostrils even before the coffee shop came into view. She pushed open the black painted door with the small square windows that were thick glass with big bubbles in the middle of each one. She felt as if she was going into a shop in the last century. She imagined she might see David Copperfield or Pickwick. A bell jingled as she opened the door. She waited for her eyes to adjust to the gloom. Looking around she saw an assortment of young people, dressed differently from their Saturday afternoon attire. There was a different atmosphere, one of anticipation, of soon moving on to a party or one of the pubs.

Tom was sitting at a table by the window. He saw her and waved. Lily felt suddenly shy and panicked and thought that maybe she shouldn't have come. She didn't know what they were going to find to talk about. Her uncertainty was followed by a pang of sadness, tinged with guilt. She realised as she walked towards Tom she'd rather just be meeting Jo. Too late, Tom was smiling at her in obvious delight. He offered to buy her coffee but she wanted to get it herself, that was half the fun of the place. Hessian sacks were tacked to the walls and each one had a country's name stamped across it. She loved to choose a coffee from Brazil or Columbia or some other exotic-sounding place and see if she could distinguish the difference; some were stronger or bitter tasting, some were smooth and rich.

Sitting down, looking at Tom, she asked, 'How are you?'

'Great, thanks. I was getting worried you weren't gonna come though.'

'It's awkward with Jo liking you so much but she assures me she's enjoying your brother's company so we'll see how it goes.'

'Yeah, they seem to be having a great time together. Carl's very keen. They've changed where we're meeting; hope you don't mind. There's a pub Jo thought you would like not far from here and it's got a beer garden.'

'If Jo thinks I'll like it, I'm sure I will.'

Tom smiled at her, seeming pleased that she didn't mind the change of plans.

'What work do you do, Tom?' She had thought of asking him this while on the bus so as not to feel self-conscious if there were too many silences.

'I'm a surveyor's help. We're building a new motorway outside of Sevenoaks and the surveyors have to make sure the roads have the right camber on them. They look through these instruments that look like yellow telescopes on a stand and take accurate measurements.

I have to set them up and hold them steady while they peer through them all day.'

'Do you like it?'

'It's all right, the pay's good and we have a laugh sometimes.'

'It doesn't sound much of a laugh being out on an open, half-made motorway in all weathers all day.' Lily didn't mean to sound doubtful but she imagined him standing outside for hours and either getting burnt by the sun or cold and wet in the wind and rain.

'Well, if it's pouring we all go into the shed and have a mug of tea till it stops. I'm the mug that has to make the tea! One day the foreman had been giving me a hard time so I said, 'Do ya wanna mug of tea, Norm?' He muttered that he did, so before he got in there I put his tin mug on the table and screwed the bottom down onto the wood and then filled it up with tea. You should have seen his face when he tried to pick it up. We all laughed till we cried.'

Lily laughed. 'I bet that didn't go down too well.'

'Nah, he went all red in the face and chased me out of the shed. I think he would have punched me but he's a fat old bastard and he couldn't catch me.'

Lily laughed even more and thought how much she liked his sense of humour. 'How come you've got a London accent?'

'All me family come from London but it was bombed so much in the war that the government offered to find homes for families in the country. My parents were given a cottage in Chitswood.'

'Do you like it there?'

'It was all right till me dad left. He's a printer for *The Times* and he still had to travel up to London every night to get the paper printed. Me mum found out later that he had been leaving an hour earlier each day than he needed and going and visiting her sister who lived down the other end of the village. Eventually me aunt got pregnant and insisted Dad leave us. So he did. Just buggered off and left us all and they got a house in London.' He shrugged, looking troubled by his dad leaving.

Lily swallowed some coffee and tried to think of what to say. Tom looked wistful. 'Did he ever come back?'

'Only when my little brother Brian drowned. He came back and told Mum he wouldn't leave her again. He stayed for a few days and then my cow of an aunt sent him a telegram saying she'd commit suicide if he didn't go back to her so he left again.'

It was all so sad and Lily looked at Tom in a different light, not just as a boy, but as a human being. Lots of questions came into her head, like why on earth would the sister have to take Tom's father away? Weren't there plenty of other men around? But she realised that would probably stir up more pain so she changed the subject. 'Let's go out and get some air, it's smoky in here.'

They got up and he took her hand. Once outside she took her hand away to look at her watch. It was already seven; she would have to catch a train home by nine thirty. 'Tom, I've only got another two hours. Can we catch a bus to meet Jo and Carl at the pub?'

'Yeah, 'course. Come on, we're meeting at the Bat and Ball. It's in Seal. It's not far but we'll get on the bus to save time.'

The pub was white with a thatched roof and looked very pretty with baskets of brightly coloured pink-and-purple petunias hanging from the eaves. Lily guessed it must be at least three hundred years old. The sun was setting behind it and the blue horizon had deep orange streaks with soft, whisper-pink clouds above it. The place was buzzing with people talking animatedly, laughing and joking, pints of lagers in their hands. Lily knew she was going to like it. It was too crowded to push their way inside, so Tom led Lily around the beer garden until they could find a space at one of the wooden tables.

'I'll get us a drink once I've found them. What would you like?'

'Shandy, thanks.'

While he was gone Lily enjoyed the warmth of the evening enveloping her like a velvet coat. She liked the laughter and the feeling of everyone coming alive in the summer after being shut up inside throughout the winter.

Tom came back bringing Jo and Carl and the drinks with him. They tried to make themselves heard above the noise; even the crickets were deafening. Jo was in good spirits and Lily, feeling relieved, soon got into the swing of things. Their conversation was varied. Lily couldn't resist asking how come some of the village names were so strange and why was Sevenoaks called Sevenoaks? Tom piped up straight away. 'There's a big manor on huge grounds called Knole Park and the geezer, you know the Lord or the Baron or whatever 'e was, planted seven oak trees. They became huge over a hundred years or so and they called the town after them. But if you think that's strange, what about a village about three miles from 'ere that's called Pratt's Bottom. How did that get its name, eh?'

They all laughed and fell into an easy banter. Lily kept looking from Jo to Tom to see if there was any awkwardness. As far as she could tell, there wasn't.

The time went in a flash and Lily had to tell them that she was sorry but she had to leave for the station. Jo and Carl decided they liked being out in the beer garden and would stay and have a few more drinks. The air was still sultry and the horizon had turned a deep purple. Tom went with Lily on the bus and walked with her onto the platform.

'I really want to see you again, Lily.'

'Tom, it's not easy, especially with the Sunday job. I'm meeting Jo next weekend and we're going to Bligh's to see the Kinks. How about I meet you there and we'll see how it goes?'

He held her tight, kissing her tenderly, and then stood back. 'That's a week away but okay then, I'll see you at Bligh's on Saturday. I wish you didn't live so far away. I've enjoyed tonight. See ya, Lily.'

She could see he wanted to say more but she was glad he'd left it at that. It was nice that he waited to see her onto the train.

Eight

'Jo, I've been seriously thinking about quitting my job at the petrol station. What do you think?'

Lily and Jo were outside getting the last warm rays of sunshine before the earth turned its back to the sun, leaving them without its warmth for the next few months.

'Fab idea. All you do at weekends is work. Why do you do it, Lily?'

'I just like nice things, Jo. When I was eleven I took over my brother's paper round delivering *The Evening Standard* and I got used to having my own money. Then when I was fourteen, my mum and I used to have screaming matches every time I wanted a pair of shoes or something. Well, I did most of the screaming, Mum just used to stand there saying she didn't have the money.' Lily felt a bit sheepish as she looked at Jo.

It had now been four weeks of getting home from work at the greengrocer's and then going up to Sevenoaks to see Tom, Jo and Carl. Always having to leave by nine thirty to get the last train home was making her feel weary. She was feeling more reluctant to leave them and miss the fun. Tom wasn't getting tired of her as she thought he might and Jo still seemed okay marking her time with Carl.

Two days later, feeling bad but with her mind made up, she told Mr and Mrs Hall that she wouldn't be able to work there anymore.

'We'll miss you, Lily, you're a good worker. If you change your mind later on, we'll be glad to have you back.'

'Thanks Mrs Hall, I'll miss you both too. I like working here, it's just that my friends live around Sevenoaks and it's hard to go out with them on Saturday nights if I work on Sundays.'

The following Saturday, Lily felt her mood lift at the prospect of getting ready to go to Bligh's to see a band knowing she could enjoy herself without having to look at her watch all the time. Getting up for the Saturday morning job was easier, knowing she could relax for the rest of the weekend after twelve o'clock. Leaving work, she felt a new lightness to her step as she walked down the hill to the station for a quick trip into Maidstone on the twelve fifteen. The train pulled into Paddock Wood; jumping out she walked across the platform and got into the connecting train.

The town was bustling with Saturday shoppers: people with heavy bags of groceries, mothers with children, and young people carrying smart bags with fancy shop names blazoned across them. Feeling wistful, she couldn't help wondering what lovely clothes were in the expensive-looking bags and looked forward to the day when she could shop in the classier stores. A rush of excitement zipped through her as she realised they would be Parisian shops. Ooh-la-la!

She hurried along a bit faster and entered into Martins. Surveying all the gorgeous dresses, skirts and tops in the small store she decisively picked out a black straight mini skirt and a sleeveless white lace cotton top. Plain but stylish, she decided, knowing she wouldn't be able to come every week now. The season had just changed into autumn anyway. She looked around the shop admiring all the displays, paid at the counter, then walked purposefully out the door and headed for the station. Passing a record store, she impulsively ducked in and bought 'Bus Stop' by the Hollies, the band they'd see at Bligh's that night.

Tom was there at the station to meet her at seven o'clock as arranged. Surprisingly she was finding she was beginning to look forward to seeing him more and more. She liked that he always did what he said he was going to.

'We could have a drink 'ere at the Station's Arms if you want, Lily, there's no need to rush.'

She felt a quiet sit-down with a drink in her hand was just what she needed. They walked into the gloomy pub and sat down in worn green leather armchairs in the corner. Tom got the drinks, a lager and a Scrumpy cider.

Lily was soon chatting animatedly, due in part to the fact that she hadn't eaten and the cider went straight to her head. They finished their drinks and reluctantly got up out of the comfy chairs, deciding it was time to go. They had to walk briskly up Tubbs hill, as they didn't want to be late but also due to the evening being cooler than usual.

'We're meeting them in the Rose and Crown for a drink.'

It was a very old pub in the High Street, a genuine Tudor building with the distinctive black wooden slats over the white walls. The heavy oak doors were so low that everyone had to duck when they went in or out. Apparently, people were smaller a couple of centuries ago. Inside the tables were dark rosewood and the carpet bright red. Horse brasses and old black-and-white pictures were hanging on the bare red brick walls. Small lamps cast a cosy, intimate light. Lily noticed the huge fireplace had big logs set in the grate in anticipation of the weather turning cold soon.

Jo was laughing when they went in and seemed to be sharing something funny with Carl. He had a baby face and humour in his crinkly eyes. He looked a lot like his mum so Lily surmised Tom must look like his dad. They looked up as Lily and Tom approached.

''Ello! Lily! Can I get you a drink?' Carl jumped up and planted a kiss on her cheek then stood back looking at her expectantly.

'Thanks, Carl, that would be lovely. I'll have half a pint of Scrumpy, please.'

'Bruv'?'

'Lager, ta!'

'Hi, Lily! How was work? Did you go to Martins and buy something new?' asked Jo.

'Oh! Can't you tell? I bought what I've got on but I made sure it was low-key as I'm going to have to mix and match a lot more now.'

'You poor thing,' Jo purred with staged sarcasm. 'I thought I hadn't seen that top before but you have so many clothes it's hard to know.'

'Come on, boys and girls, it's nearly eight. Let's get down to Bligh's before the Hollies start,' said Carl jumping up, keen to get going.

Lily downed the rest of her cider. Jo knocked back her lager and lime and they were up and ready. Tom stood back waiting for the girls to follow Carl out.

As they sauntered down the street they passed Greg, an old boyfriend of Lily's. He said hello and stared at Lily.

'Want her back do ya, Greg? You can have 'er for five quid!'

Lily was shocked at Tom being so cruel.

Greg, undeterred by Tom's taunt, whipped out his wallet and before they had time to blink, was holding a five pound note under Tom's nose! It knocked the smile off Tom's face and he quickly slid his arm around Lily's waist and started to walk away, saying, 'Nah, that's all right, mate. I'll keep 'er.'

'That was a horrible thing to say, Tom. Couldn't you have just walked by and said hello?'

Tom was quiet. Jo and Carl started playing silly buggers and laughingly changed the mood.

It was only a three-minute stroll to Bligh's. They walked in through the big double glass doors and into the dance hall. It was dark and crowded as usual, just how they liked it. There was loud music playing but everyone was looking frequently at the stage, eager for the Hollies to come on, then spontaneously bursting into shouts and whistles as they appeared on stage a couple of minutes later.

They had a great night, jigging around to the music as much as the crush of people would allow, and going to the bar in every break. It seemed everyone knew everyone else. Even Lily saw people that she knew. Kate was there of course and also the two Daves. The night just flew by and it seemed like in no time they were getting pushed along by the crowd out onto the street.

'What shall we do now?' asked Carl, sounding hopeful that they would all want to kick on to somewhere else.

No-one wanted to and Lily was relieved when everyone agreed it was getting cold so they'd rather jump on a bus and go home. Except the bus was a number 29 to Chitswood. She looked at Jo and Jo just shrugged and got on the bus. Lily felt worried. She was expecting to be leaving the boys and going back to Jo's house. It was apparent that this was the routine Jo and Carl had established over the last few weeks. Tom hugged her and seemed extremely pleased that she wasn't catching the train home tonight.

Tom's house was obscured by a twenty-foot-high hedge but as they went up the path she could see it was a lovely cottage. All the lights were out and the back door was unlocked. Carl and Jo disappeared straight up the stairs and Lily plonked down on the settee. The small room felt warm and there were some dying embers still glowing red from the fire that his mother would have sat by.

Tom sat down and put his arms around her, gently kissing her, quickly becoming aroused as his kisses became more passionate. She enjoyed it for a few moments then pushed him away. She'd played around with boys before but she always knew it would never go anywhere. But now she was going to be in his house all night and he had wanted her for weeks. She panicked at the thought of how she was going to keep it in check. 'Tom, I've told you that I'm not going to have sex with anyone until I'm sixteen and on the pill.'

'It's all right, Lily, I know. I can wait. It's only a few weeks away.' He held her again, stroking her down from her shoulders and onto her breasts, kissing her more gently now. It felt nice but Tom's breathing was getting heavy and she was getting hot. She put both hands on his chest and pushed him off her. 'I think I want to go to sleep now. Can you get me a pillow and a blanket?'

'Come and sleep in my room. You don't want me mum coming down in the morning and finding you on the couch, do you?'

It was a sobering thought.

'It'll be okay, Lily, I promise.'

She searched his face to see if he was sincere and seeing that he was, she said, 'Okay, then.'

Tom couldn't hide his look of pleasure as he took her hand and led her up the thinly carpeted stairs to his bedroom. She reluctantly got undressed but pointedly left her bra and knickers on. She was feeling anxious and annoyed that she hadn't known they would be coming back to Tom's house. Tom had thrown his clothes off on to the floor and was stark naked as he jumped into the bed. 'Come on, Lily, we'll just cuddle up and go to sleep.'

'Make sure we do, Tom, I mean it. I'm not gonna have sex with you.' She got into his bed and pulled the covers over her, feeling awkward and self-conscious. It had been a breeze when boys played around before as she was always in control. But sleeping all night in a randy boy's bed put her nerves on edge. Tom was only eighteen but he seemed very worldly to Lily.

He wrapped his arms around her and held her tight. It felt nice but then she felt hot and claustrophobic. She could feel his swelling, rock-hard cock against her leg. 'Tom! You're freaking me out. Can we just go to sleep now?'

'Sorry. It's so amazing 'aving you 'ere in my bed after all this time. I don't want to upset you. One more kiss and I'll turn over and you can go to sleep.' His words were slurring a little. He kissed her deeply and lingered longer than she felt comfortable with.

She pulled away. 'Night, Tom.'

'Night, Lily, see you in the morning.'

Incredibly, she heard him snoring in less than five minutes. So much for undying love and passion: she felt the urge to laugh out loud. But she was actually glad he'd had a few drinks. Relieved and reassured, Lily finally fell asleep.

Tom hardly moved all night but Lily was on hyper alert and was waking frequently just to check that he was asleep. He turned to her just before dawn and she awoke to feel his arms around her and his insistent cock hotly pressing against her thigh.

'Tom, turn over. Go back to sleep.'

He muttered, 'I love you, Lily.'

She pushed him gently and he rolled away from her. Her vigilance intensified but she lightly dozed until the sun brought some light into the room. Carefully getting out of bed she picked her clothes up from the floor and got dressed. Even though Jo was not normally an early riser she had agreed to Lily's whispered pleading that they leave at seven and walk back to Jo's house. Lily crept out and closed the bedroom door behind her. She carefully negotiated the stairs so as not to wake up the whole household. Once down in the lounge room and waiting for Jo, she realised it was mean of her to expect Jo to get up this early for her. A thought zipped through her: they've probably been having sex all night and Jo won't feel like getting up. Feeling guilty, she patiently waited in the Bennett's lounge room, looking around at the brown comfy sofa, the small table and chairs, the well-worn blue carpet and the fireplace. Her gaze fell onto a large framed, black-and-white photo above the mantelpiece. It had faded with time but the sweet faces of three young boys looked angelic, each with their haloes of white, blond hair. Lily walked over to look more closely in the dim light at the boys. She could see which were Tom and Carl so deduced the smallest boy must be Brian. She felt sad at what they must have all gone through with the tragedy of losing him.

She heard footsteps on the stairs and moved away from the photo in case it was Mrs Bennett. Her spirits rose when Jo put her head around the door. They smiled at each other, both glad to find each other rather than Mrs Bennett. Jo quietly pulled up the wooden latch on the back door and they crept out, down the mossy path, and, suppressing giggles, didn't say a word until they were out past the huge hedge. They both breathed out and started laughing with relief at the same time.

'Thanks, Jo. I hope I didn't spoil your sleep-in.'

'We don't usually sleep when we wake up, Lily!'

'Oh!' Lily felt the colour rush to her cheeks. But Jo seemed to be in a good mood anyway and gave Lily a hug.

'It's okay, Lily. Did you have sex with Tom?'

'No! Do you think I'm that much of a pushover? I have to say it was bloody awkward. What about their mum? Do you always have to get up early and leave before she gets up?'

'No, she's all right. It doesn't seem to bother her at all and she loves her boys, it's all she's got left. She just accepts it.'

'Do you feel awkward though, with her knowing you've been in bed with her son all night?'

'It really doesn't bother me, Lily.'

Lily was stumped for words. It all seemed so alien to her. They were passing the houses now at the other end of the village. No-one seemed to be stirring yet. Lily glanced around, wondering which house Tom's aunt, Mrs Bennett's sister, once lived in. She felt sad again for their world having been torn apart, not once but twice. What an arsehole their dad must be. She was going to say as much to Jo but now they were going down a narrow dirt path, a shortcut to Stonebridge, and there were big pink-and-black pigs snuffling their snouts up to the wire fence. Her mood changed immediately. 'Jo! Look at these gorgeous pigs.'

She stopped and began talking to them, tentatively putting her hand through the fence and stroking one behind the ear. The pig stopped still from its snuffling, seemingly enjoying it.

'Look, Jo. They're like a pet dog. I've read they're really intelligent. They're so cute.'

Jo was standing watching but not so keen to put her hand in there. 'Yeah, they look sweet but I think I'll stick to my cat for a pet. Let's get back to my place before the whole village sees us in last night's clothes. The sun's getting warm now.'

'Good point. It was a great night at Bligh's though, wasn't it? The Hollies were fabulous.'

'They made us want to dance and I had a good time. They're really good-looking.'

They were now in Stonebridge and taking another shortcut through the long grass, past the ruins of an old church. In no time they were at Jo's front gate. Lily braced herself for Mrs P's scrutiny but she was hungry and the fry-up was very appealing all of a sudden.

Nine

The following week they had a drink at the Whitehart, listened to a band at Bligh's and once again caught the bus back to Tom and Carl's house. Lily felt apprehensive but she couldn't think of a way of enticing Jo to go back to her house in Stonebridge without appearing selfish. As they had done the week before, Carl and Jo said goodnight and cleared off up the stairs to Carl's bedroom.

'Do you want to go up to bed, Lily?' said Tom hopefully.

She didn't, she wanted to put it off a bit longer. She'd had four gin and tonics at the pub to give her Dutch courage but it had only made her more wide awake. 'I'd love a hot chocolate if you have any.'

'Me mum has one every night so I know we've got some. Not sure if there'll be any milk left though.' He went into the kitchen and looked in the tiny fridge. 'Yeah, we have milk; one hot chocolate coming up.'

They sat around talking for another twenty minutes while she sipped her hot drink. Getting up to take the mug out to the sink, she knew she couldn't put off the inevitable any longer. Coming back into the room, she stayed standing and Tom quickly stood up.

'You ready for bed now?'

'Yeah, I'm getting sleepy now, so no messing around, okay?'

'Okay, Lily, I know. Come on.' He held out his hand to her and they walked up the stairs and into his bedroom.

Tom quickly pulled off all his clothes, left them in a heap on the floor and jumped into the double bed. He then lay there enjoying the show, leaving Lily feeling even more self-conscious about her body as she stood there taking her dress off but leaving her underwear on again. At least it's black and lacy, she thought, knowing that may not be a good thing but at least she looked nice. She quickly got into bed beside Tom. He immediately made a dive for her and enveloped her in his arms. He began gently stroking her arms and legs. After a while Lily felt relaxed as if she was lying on warm sand at the beach and allowing her body to bask in the gentle rays of the sun. Tom began to kiss her neck and shoulders in a tender, nuzzling way. She was getting hot and could feel stirring low in her pelvis. Without realising it, she pushed herself a little closer to him but as she felt his rigid cock burning into her thigh, she realised her mistake. 'Tom!' she gasped as she pulled away from him. 'This is getting too close.'

'It's all right, Lily, we won't go all the way but we could just play around for a while.'

He was now gently moving his thumb across her bra-covered nipple. Eventually his thumb sensuously trailed down her belly and down the inside of her thigh and under her knicker leg, gently moving to her clit and then resuming its soothing motion of moving from side to side and then around in tiny circles. She kept completely still, hardly breathing. She could feel herself getting wet and thought that she should pull away. It was a totally new experience to be able to lie back and enjoy someone else arousing her clit rather than herself. Other boys had tried the 'smash and grab' approach and she had immediately pushed their hands away, thinking that it was easy to resist having sex.

Her hips were lifting up involuntarily from the bed. Startled at her reaction she pushed Tom's hand away from her body. He seemed surprised. 'No! Tom! This is not a good idea. I want us to go to sleep now.' She pushed him away from her but before she could turn her body away from him, he kissed her with love and gentleness on her lips. 'Goodnight, Tom.'

'Okay! Okay! We'll go to sleep. Goodnight.' As he moved away from her he surprised her by saying, 'I guess you'll leave early again, Lily?'

There was wistfulness in his voice and she knew he didn't want her to leave. There was a new intimacy between them, she could feel it too. 'I have to, Tom, it's best.'

She lay there in the dark feeling relaxed and aroused at the same time. Her head reminded her that this was crazy but another voice was telling her that it felt really good. As she cooled down, logic returned, making her realise she'd have to have that talk with Jo about staying at her place on Saturday nights. As her mind went over it she began to think that going back to the Sunday morning job might be best so she wouldn't have the temptation. This seemed such a sensible idea that she immediately felt less stressed. Now Tom was softly snoring beside her, the sound reassuring her that it was now safe to go to sleep, her eyes closed.

It seemed just minutes later that she awoke to grey light coming through the gaps in the curtains. She waited until the light became brighter and then carefully slid out of the bed, picking up her clothes and putting them on. Creeping out of the room she made an inaudible sigh of relief as she quietly closed the door and tiptoed down the stairs. She waited near the back door, anxious to make her escape, worrying that Jo may sleep in. The mornings were darker now. The unwarranted thoughts provoked more anxiety and after another five minutes or so Lily was looking at the back door longingly and thinking maybe she should just go outside and wait. At that moment she heard a creak of someone coming down the stairs. She waited expectantly, praying it was Jo, but saw instead the sleepy, crumpled face of Mrs Bennett. She looked so adorable, short and round with a pink dressing gown and a hair net making a line across her forehead. Lily felt her shoulders relax.

''Ello, love, are you waiting for Jo? Shall I make us a cup of tea?'

As she began filling the kettle Jo put her head around the door. Taking in the situation, she smiled brightly at Mrs Bennett, saying, 'Good morning, Mrs Bennett, how are you today?'

'I'm all right, love, what about you? Sleep all right? Lily's going to have a cup of tea with me, would you like one?'

Looking at Lily with raised eyebrows and a smile, Jo turned and said, 'Yes, please, that'd be lovely.'

'Sit down then and I'll bring it in a jiffy. I've got some biscuits with jam centres; we'll have those too, eh?'

Within five minutes the three of them were sitting around the coffee table, sipping hot tea and munching on the sweet biscuits. Mrs Bennett had pulled off her hairnet revealing her blonde-and-greying permed hair. She seemed to be relishing the company. 'What are you two up to today then?'

Lily piped up, 'It's our exams soon so we mainly study on Sundays.'

'That's very good, O levels, are they? I wish my Tom had stuck it out, he's so brainy but he wouldn't stay at that posh school. Carl neither.' She trailed off wistfully.

Lily realised she really liked Tom's mum. She had seen her before a couple of times when she and Jo were in Woolworths. Mrs Bennett worked on the deli counter and even though she was only about five feet tall, she seemed just high enough to use the meat slicing machine without standing on tiptoe.

'Well, that was a nice start to the morning but we'd better be going now, Mrs Bennett. Hope you have a lovely day,' Jo said as she got up and started to take the cups out. Lily enthusiastically agreed and helped by taking their plates to the kitchen.

'All right, dears, you're good girls and I hope you do well in the exams. Expect I'll see you both soon.' She stood up from her armchair as they waved on their way out the door.

'Are you all right, Lily?'

'Yeah, I'm all right. Mrs Bennett is lovely; I can see why you like her so much.'

They walked in silence for a while. Lily was trying to get ready to bring up the subject of them going back to Jo's house from now on but she chickened out. She looked up and saw they were already at the other end of the village. As they went down the dirt path she could see the pigs weren't up against the fence today. It had rained hard in the night and they were happily lying around in the mud. They looked contented and it brought a smile to her face.

'Look, Jo! Aren't they cute?'

Jo looked but she didn't share Lily's love of animals to the same degree. 'Yeah, funny how pigs love wallowing in mud, don't you think?'

'I dunno, I've read that wealthy women pay loads of money to be covered in mud so it may have its merits!'

They giggled at the thought of ageing women trying to stay young by paying to be plastered in mud. The sun started to warm them and they pushed on a bit faster.

Ten

L ily and Tom left Bligh's Hotel around midnight and caught the late bus back to his mother's house. Jo and Carl had gone on to some club near Bromley. Summer had long passed into autumn and the nights were getting dark and damp. There was a feeling of anticipation now of getting into Tom's bed and resuming the intimacy and the passion she had felt the week before. Lily knew she was playing with fire but a genie had been let out of the bottle.

With no polite preliminaries, they went up the narrow stairs to Tom's bed. The room was cold like winter and they hurriedly pulled off their clothes and jumped under the covers. Tom reached for her and enfolded her in his arms. She reasoned if they could just play around like the week before for another few weeks, she would be on the pill and they could have sex. Tom was kissing her and his lips were warm and soft. As he began gently stroking her arms and thighs, Lily gradually let go and relaxed. Slowly and deliberately Tom unfastened her bra. This time as he stroked her nipples she felt them harden immediately, the intensity magnified by skin on skin. His hand slowly slid down her stomach to between her thighs and she held her breath with the anticipation of it feeling as good as it did before. He seemed to have infinite patience as he slowly played with her clit. His mouth was now ever so gently sucking her nipple and after a while, she started to lose all reason as her mind shut off and she could only feel her body. Becoming hot and restless, she started to wriggle and arched her back a little. At that moment Tom easily slid his fingers into her wet and slippery cunt. Her eyes flew open and with a knee-jerk reaction she pushed his hand away. Lying there with Tom holding her tight, his rock-hard cock quivering in anticipation on her thigh, she felt her soft, inner folds were pulsing with the same anticipation. She had to have him inside her. Surely just this once would be okay. She started to pull him on top of her. Much to her surprise, Tom hesitated, and said, 'Are you sure, Lily?'

'Yes! Yes! I want to feel you inside of me.'

He rolled his body slightly and slid inside her. She gasped; his cock felt very large and very hard, yet hot and silky. He was slowly moving in and out of her. Holding him tight, Tom started moving firmly and rhythmically inside of her. She was getting hotter; her clit that was already aroused to the point of orgasm before he entered her was swelling up and eagerly seeking the weight and the friction on it. He began thrusting in and out, faster and faster. She couldn't hold back; she arched her back, thrusting her pelvis forward, and started to shudder. Tom stiffened and cried out and she felt his hot fluid shoot into her. She was beyond caring. They both collapsed and became limp in each other's arms. Within seconds, thoughts were trying to attract her attention. She pushed Tom off her and said, 'Tom! What have we done?'

He sounded sleepy as he answered. 'It'll be all right, Lily. We'll make sure it doesn't happen again.'

He held her, wanting to allay her fears but he slipped into sleep. Lily felt annoyed he could go to sleep after what had just happened.

Her body felt warm and pliable but her head was now shrieking at her for being so reckless. She tried to rationalise but a familiar feeling of resignation came over her. The feeling that something has happened and now there's nothing you can do about it. She found herself staring into the pitch black of the room. She could see a cluster of tiny, twinkling, white lights. They were slowly moving and delicately changing shape. She screwed her eyes shut tight and then opened them again. They were definitely there, just above where she knew the door would be. They looked mystical. Deep down, she knew what they were. Since puberty she sometimes had premonitions. She was so fascinated by this secret world that every year she couldn't wait until the fair rolled into her village so she could go to the mysterious fortune-teller in a tiny striped tent. She would have dark hair and dark eyes and wear a brightly coloured scarf tied around her head and be sitting with a pack of Tarot cards and a crystal ball in front of her on the small, round table. Her thoughts screamed at her to stop daydreaming and go to the bathroom and wash herself.

Quickly getting out of bed, her silver St. Christopher necklace fell from around her neck to the floor. Her hand flew to her mouth; she knew she was definitely pregnant. Bending to pick up her necklace in the dark, she felt she was watching herself from above. St. Christopher is the patron Saint of safety but it was too late; even he couldn't save her now. She fumbled through the dark and found the door handle. Fearing the unbelievable had happened, she sat on the loo and peed for as long as she could and then looked around for something to wash her insides out. The corner of a towel would have to do. After soaking it, she furiously washed herself over and over again.

Back in Tom's bed she felt claustrophobic as if she was buried alive in an Egyptian tomb and desperately needed the action of digging herself out. She was sure she would never be able to sleep, until at last sleep took her without her knowledge.

Lily awoke to shards of early morning light coming in through the curtains. She lay there for a moment, then suddenly remembered what she had done the night before. Panic seized her, making her chest feel tight. She leapt out of bed, grabbed her crumpled clothes off the floor, yanked them on and hurried down the stairs. Jo must have heard her because within minutes, before Lily had got her coat on, she came down into the lounge.

'You're noisy this morning. Are you okay?'

'Yeah, I really want to get going. Can we go back to your house now?'

'Suits me.'

As usual, Lily was walking ahead, her long legs striding out, and Jo was reminding her to slow down. But it was a half-hour walk to Jo's house and she wanted to get there as fast as possible.

'You're walking funny. You're not pregnant, are you?'

Lily stopped in her tracks, thinking, oh dear God! I must be pregnant, that's three things now. 'Don't be silly, Jo. It's just that I'm starving and I'm looking forward to your mum's egg-and-bacon breakfast.'

They walked down the road and out of Chitswood, turning onto the dirt path, past the pigs in their field of mud. Lily didn't notice them today. Passing the modern houses, some showing signs of people stirring on this brisk, grey morning, they crossed the main road into Stonebridge and took the shortcut past the old church. The long grass was wet with dew and normally Lily complained about it feeling unpleasant on her legs and making her shoes wet. Today she didn't care. They chatted intermittently about the night before and the club that Jo had been to. Lily didn't feel like breakfast or seeing Mrs P but she had to have an excuse for her need to hurry.

After breakfast they talked about school and home-work but then Lily made excuses to get going. She assured Jo that she didn't need her to walk down to the bus stop with her and that she should get stuck into her homework as it would be exams soon. She needed to be alone with her thoughts. ''Bye, Jo, see you tomorrow.'

Jo looked at her quizzically but shrugged her acceptance.

Walking down the road, Lily knew the first thing she had to do was to make an appointment with a doctor and find out if she really was pregnant or if it was just her overactive imagination. She wondered how long she would have to wait before a doctor would know and she felt the wait would kill her. A little voice said, if your dad doesn't kill you first! She withdrew into herself and felt serious and solitary. This wasn't a bad thing. From a very young age Lily had always had to cope with the serious things in life alone. It was what she knew best and she felt stronger this way. If she coped with things alone no-one else could take control and tell her what to do. Or worse, shout or hit her. She would have to work this out.

Waiting for the bus, a memory swiftly surfaced of when she was five years old. Her mother had told her, 'Lily, you're going to stay with your Aunty Mary for a few days.' Lily thought this was odd as she had never stayed there before. She felt worried. It wasn't that she didn't like Aunty Mary; she was a bit fussy but had always been kind. And she liked her cousin Caroline, although she didn't get to see her that often. The two families would catch the train to go on the Sunday school outing once a year to Folkestone beach. They took her to the village library with them every fortnight and they would see each other in church if there was a special occasion. Uncle Cyril was a nice, gentle man.

He was always whistling and cheerful and he allowed them to go into his signal box at the station where he worked and they would watch as he pulled huge levers to move the railway tracks, directing the trains. He was a welcome change from her moody father. She remembered how even at that young age, she wondered if she had been particularly bad and maybe her parents didn't want her anymore.

It had been nice to be able to play with Caroline every day but on the day they said they were taking her home she had been very glad. She had run in through the back door into the kitchen, looking for her mother. Not finding her she had ran on through the kitchen and then into the lounge, calling, 'Mummy, Mummy.' She'd stopped in her tracks as she rounded the corner and had seen her mother cradling a huge baby with a head of curly, blond hair. She had glanced up at Lily but was absorbed with her new baby. A wave of sadness had engulfed Lily. They had replaced her while she was away. She had felt she wasn't wanted anymore. She felt a pain in her heart and had turned away to go up to her room to nurse her sadness and abandonment. She decided that day that she would manage alone then, if no-one wanted her. They hadn't mentioned a new baby was arriving. They had kept it from her.

Lily carried with her from that moment on the feeling that she was not wanted, not good enough and was easily replaced. She got sick soon after and Dr Ferris said that she had a collapsed lung and pneumonia and had to go in an ambulance to hospital. Evidently the hospital was a long way away, Ashford, as her parents only came to visit her on Sunday afternoons. Once they didn't even come to see her then. The nurse explained to her that the train tracks were being repaired and the trains weren't running. The feelings of despair and abandonment were a great weight inside of her. They had forgotten about her. She had been there six weeks. Hardening her resolve and forcing herself out of her reverie, Lily decided that if she could get through that when she was five, she could get through anything. The bus arrived and distracted her train of thoughts that were leading her into grief. She got off one bus and straight onto another that was leaving for the station and her train home.

Eleven

For two agonising weeks Lily dragged herself out of bed and went to school every day, acting as if nothing had happened. She rang Mr and Mrs Hall and asked if they still needed someone to work on Sundays and was relieved to find that they did, giving her an excuse to tell Jo and Tom that she couldn't stay overnight. They appeared confused by Lily's strange behaviour. Tom asked her if she was upset and was this her way of avoiding sex until she could get on the pill. Lily wasn't even thinking about how it looked to everyone else, she was only concerned with getting her nightmare sorted out.

Finally, she reasoned that enough time had gone by and she could make an appointment with a doctor. She found one in Tonbridge and made an appointment for Wednesday afternoon after school. On the dreaded day she left school early saying she had a dentist appointment. Walking down the hill slowly, her body felt heavy as if filled with lead. She reached the busy High Street and began looking at all the numbers on the doors until she found 335. Willing herself to open the door and enter, she gave her name to a young girl, not much older than herself. The waiting room was full of mothers with coughing children and with very old people. She prayed her turn would be soon.

It seemed an interminable amount of time before her name was called. She went in and looked across a cluttered mahogany desk at a tall, thin man around forty. He wore a white shirt and a royal blue tie. Thick brown hair flopped over his forehead giving him a Cambridge, old boys' look. He set his unusually green eyes on hers and said, 'Have a seat, Miss Davis. I'm Dr Morrison, how can I help you?'

'I told reception I had stomach pains but the truth is I think I may be pregnant.'

'How old are you?'

'I'll be sixteen on the 1st of December. Trouble is, Dr Morrison, I may only be two and a half weeks gone. Can you tell this early?'

He studied her face, as if to decide whether she may be wasting his time. 'With an internal we can but we'll follow up with a blood test just to be sure. Let's get you up on the table and have a look. Go behind the curtain and remove your underpants and let me know when you're ready.'

Lily did as she was asked, all the time praying that he would find that she was not pregnant. She tried not to squirm as he pushed around inside her. The examination took less than two minutes. She tried to read his face but his expression was grave. Lily stemmed her panic, consoling herself that doctors always practised a deadpan look.

'Get dressed and come and sit down when you're ready.'

She hastily put her underwear back on and with her heart feeling heavy and tears pricking her eyes, she sat meekly in the chair waiting for her sentence to be announced.

'You are pregnant, Lily. Before you leave I will get nurse to take your blood but I have no doubt.'

With a sharp intake of breath, Lily managed to control herself and took the news stoically. The doctor was officious but took the time to ask her what she was going to do. Did she want to keep the baby? Would she consider adoption? He assured her this was a popular option these days. Or was she thinking of marrying the boy? She told him that she needed time to think about what she would do. Her mind was racing in several directions at once. She found it almost impossible to hold herself together, wanting to fall to the floor and give up the fight. He gave her a card with the name and phone number of a social worker and advised her sombrely that she needed to phone her as this was a very common problem with young girls and the social worker knew how to help. Lily held on to the card tightly and said in a shaky voice, 'Thank you, Dr Morrison.'

After stepping out of the room she was ushered into another to have the blood test, all the time resisting the urge to break into sobs and run out the door. She hadn't wanted to believe it was true. She'd hoped and prayed every day that she was mistaken. She desperately needed to be by herself so she could break down and cry but had to get the train home first.

Barely holding back her tears on the journey and the walk past the shops in Highden, she finally raced up the path and in the back door. Flinging her bag on the kitchen floor, she ran up the stairs into her bedroom, slamming the door behind her. She threw herself onto her bed and cried and cried. She wanted to open her mouth and scream her lungs out but instead she had to keep her face in the pillow and not make too much noise. She asked herself, how she could have been so stupid and what would she do now. She sobbed and felt her heart must be breaking, it was hurting so much. Her mind was whirling so fast it felt like her head might burst. She asked herself angrily, how could she, Lily Davis, with all her carefully laid plans to flee from her parents' home and start a new life in Paris with her best friend, end up like this. The stark reality was that she was not even sixteen and her life hadn't begun yet. Her sobs subsided and she was suddenly icy calm. Sitting up and blowing her nose, she wiped the tears from her eyes and started to think more clearly. She ran her hands through her hair and found it was as wet as her face. She knew her eyes must be red and swollen but no-one else was home so they wouldn't see.

She had to be logical. What choices did she have? She went through them one by one. Abortion was not an option. Once it's done she knew she may never get over it and it could haunt her every day for the rest of her life. They were illegal anyway and some women died from them. She felt like a coward but knew she couldn't risk it. It was too final. Maybe she and Tom could get married and keep the baby? No! She didn't love him and there was no point in making two mistakes. She imagined this scenario and shuddered. It would be her worst nightmare to get married so young. The option of being a single mother was next but the thought chilled her soul. She knew with conviction she would never do this. She'd have to continue living at home and her child would be subjected to the same violence and fear that she had had to cope with all her life. She would eventually start going out again and her child would be left in the care of her parents. She finally decided adoption to be the most sensible option. There would be a married couple that had been longing for a baby, maybe for years but for some reason they couldn't conceive. What a cruel joke. She couldn't even get away with having sex once and she got pregnant. Lily felt herself harden as bitterness crept in. She shrugged it off. No time to feel sorry for herself. This felt like the right decision: the baby would be loved and have a good life and she would be able to pick up the pieces and get on with her life again.

Reality dawned on her. She would have to go into an unmarried mothers' home, the ones she'd read about often in the newspaper. The reports had said words to the effect that there was an epidemic of young girls getting pregnant. It was true that the 1960s had brought 'free love'; it was exciting but the birth control pill was only freely available to girls over sixteen. The girls had a sense of freedom but there were new expectations from the boys. Girls all over England had been paying the price; now, Lily thought, I'm paying the price. Tears trickled down her cheeks again but she wiped them angrily away. She had to make that phone call to the social worker now, before anyone else got home. Blowing her nose noisily, she walked slowly with heavy steps to the bathroom. Splashing her face with the icy water, she then went down to use the phone at the bottom of the stairs. Snatching the card out of her pocket, she dialled the number.

A voice sounding middle-aged and disapproving said, 'Maidstone Community Centre.'

Lily cringed, wondering if this person was the social worker. 'My name is Lily Davis; can I speak to Miss Lindsay, please?'

'What is it in relation to?'

'I need to find out about having a baby adopted.'

'I see.'

Feeling paranoid, she was sure there was a sneer in the receptionist's voice. Despair swept through her again; she took a breath and said, 'Dr Morrison has given me her number.'

'Hold the line then, miss, and I'll put you through.'

Lily exhaled with relief. A young and kindly voice came on the line. 'Miss Lindsay here, how can I help you?'

Lily, bolstered by the sound of the person on the other end of the line, blurted, 'My name is Lily Davis and I'm pregnant. Dr Morrison has given me your card.'

'I see, and how old are you, Lily?'

'I'm nearly sixteen.'

'Have you told your parents?'

'No, and I'm not going to until I've got this all worked out. My father would beat me and my mother wouldn't know how to cope and neither of them would be of any help at all. Can you help me?'

'Yes, I can definitely help you. Can you come to see me here in the centre?'

'Yes. When can I come in?'

How far along are you?'

Lily felt anxious, she couldn't tell the woman that it was only two weeks so she lied and said, 'About two months but I need to get a plan so I know what I'm to do.'

'Okay, Lily, can you get here at two p.m. tomorrow and we'll see what we can do?'

Without hesitating, she said, 'Yes.'

She got the address then ran back up the stairs and into the bathroom to sort out her face and hair so as to look normal when her mum got home. That done she went back into her room and got out of her school clothes and into a jumper and jeans, lay back down on the bed and stared up at the ceiling. Sadness was an old familiar friend. So was feeling alone. In the past she'd console herself with music but she didn't feel like playing her sad records that she had been buying one by one since she was thirteen. She had liked the state of melancholy that she could share with them. The first record she ever bought was 'Hello Heartache, Goodbye Love' by Little Peggy March. How she loved that song. Little Peggy's voice was so full of feeling and Lily would sing along as though her heart would break. Today though, it just might.

When she came home with the single record in 1963, they didn't even have a record player. She begged and pleaded with her older brother Simon, who was working at his first job by then, to buy one. He, being stubborn and old-fashioned like their father, refused. A year later, undeterred, Lily came home from spending her earnings on an LP. She was so excited; she'd heard the song on *Top of the Pops* called 'Route 66' by The Rolling Stones. The music was like nothing she had heard before. She had to have it. It cost more because it was a much bigger record with several songs on it. She asked Simon again if he would buy a record player and showed him what she had bought. This time his interest was engaged as he also watched the new pop program. 'But how much are they, Lily?' he asked with a frown, yet not being able to resist looking at the front and back of the album cover.

She'd told him she'd had a good look in the shops in Maidstone and if they bought the basic one, just a box with a lid and not fancy with polished wood and all that, they're only about twelve pounds. She watched her brother seriously considering this even though it would have probably been a week's pay, but then he had said, 'Okay, we'll get one.'

Lily had stood still for a moment as though suspended in time. She wasn't used to getting what she wanted and it was as if her ears weren't working. But then his answer had burst through and she literally jumped for joy! Simon had laughed at her reaction. They rarely laughed together. They were both cautious at home so as not to incite their father's anger.

Simon was slim and good-looking with chiselled features, blue eyes fringed with long, thick black eyelashes that Lily wanted for herself. He worked hard and seemed very responsible as far as Lily could tell. She didn't feel she knew him well so it was very exciting when they had caught the train together to Maidstone the following Saturday and bought the record player.

It was a simple wooden box covered in turquoise-and-cream-coloured vinyl. It had snazzy gold flecks through the vinyl and a shiny gold clasp that held the lid shut. Inside there was a turntable and an arm with a needle that you would put onto the record. The speaker was in the bottom with big cream-and-gold plastic knobs that could be turned to make it louder or deeper in sound. Lily and Simon had thought that it was the most fabulous thing they had ever owned. From that day on Lily felt like she had a friend in their house, the record player. Most weeks she would buy something new. It made all her efforts at working so many jobs worthwhile. She bought Roy Orbison's 'Only the Lonely', Brenda Lee's 'All Alone Am I' and sometimes records from the latest bands like The Beatles or Gerry and the Pacemakers. Simon would buy gutsier records like 'House of the Rising Sun' by The Animals.

Now she felt a wave of affection for Simon. The record player had been a godsend but she wouldn't be able to tell him about being pregnant. She would wag school tomorrow and see what Miss Lindsay could suggest.

Twelve

Feeling apprehensive, Lily walked up to the reception desk. She heard the condescending voice of the receptionist before she could see her face. She looked up as Lily approached the desk. She wasn't as old as Lily had expected, probably in her early fifties, but her face was deeply lined with pinched features that belied her disposition. Her eyes were small and grey and her lips a thin line. The name on her badge was Miss Greaves.

'Can I help you?'

'I'm Lily Davis and I'm here to see Miss Lindsay.'

'Take a seat down the corridor. She will come for you when she's ready.' She inclined her head to the right and then bowed her head and shoulders back to some task, revealing some thinning of her greying, permed hair. Lily was dismissed. She looked down the corridor and saw three blue vinyl chairs along the wall. Being empty, she felt relieved that she wouldn't have long to wait. Sitting down in the chair nearest the door, Lily kept glancing nervously at her Timex. It was five to two. The minutes ticked slowly by. The door opened and a much younger woman appeared. Miss Lindsay had shoulder-length, fair hair. She was about five foot five inches tall with a slight frame, very pretty and wore no makeup. Her pale features lit up as she smiled at Lily. 'Lily Davis? Come in.'

Lily jumped up and followed her into her office, keen to get this over with.

'Take a seat here, Lily. Can I get you a cup of tea or a glass of water?'

As Lily looked around the room she felt she was in someone's cosy home. There were paintings on the walls, knick-knacks on the small desk and the chairs were old tan-leather armchairs. She quickly sat on one, declining the offer of something to drink. Miss Lindsay sat opposite her. 'Now, Lily, take your time and tell me about your situation.' She sat back in her armchair as if she had all the time in the world to listen to Lily's story.

After Lily had explained her situation and how she still couldn't believe she was actually pregnant, Miss Lindsay asked, 'From what you've told me it sounds like you don't want to keep the baby so are you thinking adoption would be best?'

'Yes. I've gone over all the options and I feel adoption is the best answer.'

'I see, and you feel quite sure about this, Lily?'

'Yes, I do. My mind is made up.'

'When is your sixteenth birthday?'

'December the first.'

'I will take down all your details in a moment but I need to explain to you first what will happen if you go down that path. You will only be able to go into a home when you are six months pregnant. This means that you have to face your family for the first six months of your pregnancy. There is one close by outside of Maidstone that I can book you into.'

All the while she was talking she kept a steady gaze on Lily's face, assessing her reaction. After a pause she continued. 'You're not alone, Lily, thousands of girls are getting caught out, not realising how high the chance of pregnancy is with unprotected sex. Some desperately want to keep their child but their parents won't allow it. There are scores of unmarried mothers' homes across England and they are all full. You will have the baby and after three days the baby will be given to the adoptive parents that have already been found. Does that all sound okay with you?'

'Will the parents be kind and decent people?'

'Oh, yes, definitely. We have a long list of couples who are unable to have children, and there is a process of investigating the couples to make sure they are good people with a solid background. Now if you're sure this is best for you and your child I will take down all your details. How far along are you exactly?'

Lily looked at the young social worker who was earnestly doing her best to help her and felt awkward that she had to confess she had lied. 'It's actually only three weeks but it has been confirmed by Dr Morrison.

I'm sorry, Miss Lindsay, but I knew if I told you the truth on the phone you would have put me off and I wouldn't have been able to cope with this on my own for much longer.'

If Miss Lindsay was surprised she didn't show it. Lily ploughed on, wanting to get her point of view across before Miss Lindsay turned her away. 'You see, I have to have a solid plan in place before I can tell my parents. My father will fly into a rage and beat me and my mother will not know what to do and will fall to pieces.' Tears ran down her cheeks as she implored her to understand.

'I understand what you're saying, Lily, but the point is, up until three months there is the possibility of a miscarriage and therefore I can't book places until that time has passed.'

Lily felt agitated and distressed. With a sense of urgency, she cut in with, 'Unless I know that I have a home to go into I won't be able to cope. My parents don't support me in anything. I have no-one else to turn to.' She was pleading now.

After a brief silence, Miss Lindsay said, 'I can see your home life is difficult so I will make an exception in your case and I will reserve the place for you in Craigmore. Now let's get down to all your details.'

Relief flooded through Lily; she would have a plan to anchor her. She liked Miss Lindsay and felt she could trust her. She left feeling that the last part of her pregnancy was taken care of, she now had to think through how to handle the next five months.

She walked slowly down to the bus depot. There was no hurry but she wanted to ring Jo before her mother got home. She stopped in her tracks as she tried to imagine what Jo was going to feel about this. Reality hit her: she wasn't the only one to be affected by this; there was Jo and Tom to consider too. She felt panic again. Telling others was going to be the worst part. She couldn't tell Jo on the phone. In fact, she should tell Tom first. She was seeing Tom on Saturday afternoon, she would tell him then and tell Jo soon after. She knew Jo was going to hate her. Tears sprang into her eyes again. She didn't want to lose her friend but she knew she already had.

Once Lily was home, she lay on her bed and started to plan the next five months. She would start to show in three months and school ended in December, ironically soon after her sixteenth birthday. She reckoned that she would be able to finish school and do her exams. She would have to tell her parents in another month. She knew she would have to ask her mum to tell her father when she wasn't around. He wouldn't lash out at her mother but she had to admit to herself she was too scared to tell her father that she was pregnant. Every so often when she got home from Maidstone on a Saturday afternoon after having spent her earnings on a new dress or blouse, he had dragged his eyes from the television and had told her that she wasn't to come back home if she got herself pregnant. As if wearing these new fashions meant everyone was living a life of sin. Now she knew he would think he was right. Tears poured out of Lily's eyes as she wondered how she could have abandoned all her big plans to live an extraordinary life and end up like this at fifteen years and ten months old. She'd sold herself out. She reasoned there had been other boys who had been keen on her but she was never tempted to have sex with them. Greg had loved her but she was sure you can't make yourself love someone just because they love you. Yet she had been influenced by that love. Tom's love for her shone out of him. It didn't seem to be infatuation. She asked herself whether she had sex with Tom because she felt loved. In a lightbulb moment she saw that having intercourse is the closest you can get to someone and that's probably why everyone wants to have sex all the time!

Lily had eagerly read books by Jung and Freud when she was fourteen, trying to figure out why human beings do certain things that ensure their success but others do things that put them on a path of failure. Carl Jung proposed that we have a shadow self that follows us around. The shadow is made up of all the parts of ourselves that we don't want to own up to. The more we disown them though, the more they run our lives as we keep attracting other people into our lives who show us that part until we love it and own it. A common one, the book said, is disowned anger as most families think it is an undesirable trait. Lily knew anger was acceptable in her family but she reasoned fun and laughter were not. Freud talked about the sub-conscious running us and lots about our hang- ups to do with our father or mother that she couldn't even begin to understand. She'd struggled to make sense of it. She couldn't see how what she'd read could help her now. She wanted to know, why Tom, why now and why did it have to be the one that Jo wanted that loved her. Confusion made her ask herself if perhaps she did love Tom. She felt she didn't. It was a mess. She sent up a silent prayer: Dear God, please help.

Thirteen

For the rest of the week Lily pretended that everything was normal. She went to school and talked with her friends and planned to see Jo at Bligh's on Saturday. She was shocked to be voted class captain that week. She never thought they would vote for her. She was a loner and only let some people in. She felt honoured yet sad that they were unaware she would be leaving at the end of term. She knew she'd have to lie and tell them that she had a job in London. She held back tears, the enormity of what was happening to her coming to the forefront of her mind like a slap in the face. A lot of the time she'd forget. It didn't seem real. She didn't think in terms that a baby was growing inside of her. She looked normal. But the light had gone out of her eyes and her face looked pinched. She wasn't laughing spontaneously with the girls anymore. Jo gave her odd looks. She couldn't wait to tell Jo the truth; it was killing her to keep this from her best friend.

Saturday came and Lily dragged herself out of bed and washed and dressed to go to work at the fruit shop. It wasn't hard work, it was normally fun, but everything seemed like an effort now. After the shop closed Lily had no intention of jumping on a train to Maidstone and going to see what clothes Martins had this week. What would be the point? She would be too fat for them soon anyway.

The coffee smell didn't seem so fabulous when it met Lily's nose halfway down the cobbled street. She pushed the door open; even the bell that had seemed enchanting before seemed shrill now. Tom was there, talking to some guys, probably enjoying a discussion on existentialism or some such thing. She'd discovered that he was very intelligent with an exceptionally high IQ and had gained a scholarship to Cranbrook Boarding School when he was thirteen. But the boys had teased him mercilessly about his accent and upbringing. He ran away and had refused to go back. She felt a pang of sadness at what she was about to tell him.

'Hi, Tom!'

Tom swung around and his face lit up as he saw her standing there. 'Lily! Do you want a coffee? This is Ian and Jeremy; they're studying art at uni.'

'Hi, Ian! Hi, Jeremy! Nice to meet you.' She turned to Tom saying, 'You know what, Tom, if it's all right with you, I really need to walk around and get some sunshine. Is that okay?'

'Yeah, sure, let's do that. Catch ya' later, Ian, Jeremy.'

They walked out and Tom held her hand, anxiously scanning her face. 'What's wrong, Lily?'

'Tom, I'm not feeling too good. I'd like to just go straight up to Jo's place and have a rest on her bed before we go out tonight.'

''Course! Why don't I take you up to Stonebridge on the bus and then I'll see you tonight at Bligh's?'

It was a good plan but she had to tell him before she told Jo. 'Yeah, great.'

The walk to the bus depot took only a few minutes and the Stonebridge bus rumbled in soon after. They clambered up the stairs to the back seat on the top deck. Seeing there were only a few people up there, as soon as the bus took off, Lily blurted out, 'Tom, I'm pregnant!'

He turned around and put his arms around her. Looking into her eyes and wiping away the tears running down her face, he lovingly said, 'It's all right, Lily, you'll be sixteen soon and then we can get married!'

She felt an irrational burst of anger surge through her. 'I wouldn't marry you if you were the last man on earth!' She didn't know where that came from but she knew she was blaming Tom for her being pregnant. His face crumpled as if he might cry but she didn't feel she wanted to try and make it better.

'I've seen a doctor and a social worker. I'm booked into an unmarried mothers' home and I will have the baby adopted.'

He looked as though she had punched him. Lily felt she couldn't care how he felt; she had to take care of herself right now. More cautiously now, Tom said, 'Then what about us, Lily?'

'I can't see you anymore. I have to deal with this alone. I'll have to get a job for a few months after I leave school and pretend everything's normal for the sake of keeping up appearances to the neighbours. After that I'll go into the home for three months. I don't want to embarrass Mum and Dad.'

'Have you told them yet?'

'No! I wanted to tell you first, and then Jo. I'll tell them about a month before I leave school. Jo's gonna hate me.' Fresh tears poured down Lily's cheeks. She became aware that people were turning to look at them.

The bus had stopped a few times and she looked out of the window to see if they were in Stonebridge yet. He put his arms around her again. 'Lily, I feel bad that I've made you pregnant but I love you and I don't want to lose you. You're angry with me now but if you change your mind I'll be here for you.'

The bus pulled in at her stop and they both got out. Tom hugged her. Lily was holding back tears and she could see that Tom was too. What else could she do? She didn't want to get married so there was nowhere else to go with them. She pulled away saying, 'Goodbye, Tom,' and started to walk up the hill to Jo's house. Tom turned and went the other way, walking in the direction of Chitswood. Lily dragged herself along the street feeling utterly miserable. Something made her stop and glance back and Tom had stopped and was looking back at her. She turned her head and increased her pace; the worst bit was still to come.

As she knocked on the front door, Lily tried to compose her face into something bright and expectant. Mrs P opened the door and seemed to frown as she saw Lily. Lily couldn't be sure. Opening the door, she stepped back, seemingly resigned to the fact that Lily would be coming in anyway. 'She's up in her room,' she said, and inclined her head that way as if to verify it.

'Okay, Mrs P, thanks.' Lily was relieved to be able to go up the stairs and not suffer any more scrutiny.

She knocked on Jo's door. 'Jo, it's me!'

She heard Jo's voice say, 'Come in then,' sounding exasperated at having to state the obvious. Jo was lying on her bed reading a magazine, propped up on pillows. She took one look at Lily and said, 'What on earth's wrong? You look like your cat died!'

Lily slumped on the end of the bed and looked imploringly into her friend's eyes for understanding. 'Jo, I'm pregnant.'

Jo's eyes darkened momentarily and then, as if by will, she brightened them again and said, 'Oh, Lily, what a rotten thing to happen. What are you going to do?'

Through her tears, Lily told Jo that she'd gone through all the options and settled on adoption.

'Why don't you have an abortion and get it over with?'

Lily wearily turned her head and said, 'Jo, they're not even legal and it's hard to explain but I just don't think I could live with it. It's not religious or anything but I think maybe I'm a coward and I'm scared it will haunt me till the day I die. I've thought about it a lot, believe me. I figure there must be plenty of married couples out there who have dreamed of having a baby, maybe for years, and because of fate or something, they haven't been able to have one. They would be mature and have money. The baby would have a wonderful life with people who loved it and could give it everything it could possibly want. This just feels best, Jo.' She said all this haltingly, gulping in air and wiping her nose and eyes with her hand.

Jo had a look of concentration on her face as if finding it hard to understand her. 'Have you told Tom?'

'I did just before I came here.'

'How'd he take it?'

'He seemed really upset and I told him I don't want to see him anymore.'

Jo searched Lily's face. 'Why not?'

'You know, Jo, it's been difficult from the beginning and I never thought it would get as far as me having sex with him, let alone getting pregnant. I've always been torn between loving you and worrying about your feelings but wanting the love and the tenderness that he's shown me. Now I guess I feel angry with him and the whole situation and I just don't want him near me.'

Through her anguish and her sobs Lily was dimly aware that this seemed to please Jo but she couldn't care about that now. The sobs took over and Jo got up and put her arms around her.

'It's just bad luck. God knows why you don't just get rid of it! I've heard of a few girls having "back street" abortions now. They all survived as far as I know.'

'No, Jo, it's not an option.'

'Okay then, but once you've had it adopted everything will be all right again.'

'But I'll have to leave school, get some poxy job and then go into an unmarried mothers' home for three months. And we won't be able to move to Paris.' She dissolved into sobs again.

'We may still be able to go, Lily, especially if you can still study those few months and get your A levels. I have to stay on at school and get mine.'

It seemed to Lily that it may be still possible after all. Jo's words were comforting. Her hysteria quietened to a whimper as Jo gave Lily a hanky and told her to blow her nose. Lily smiled through the tears. It was nice, Jo taking care of her. It was such a relief finally being able to tell Jo her plight. She felt exhausted from all the crying and lay down on the bed beside Jo in companionable silence.

After a while Jo said, 'Do you want to go to Bligh's tonight? We can do something else if you want.'

Lily felt a weight go off her shoulders. She'd wondered how on earth she was going to put on a brave face for the pub.

'We could go to the cinema instead if you like.'

'That sounds a lot easier. Are you sure that's all right with you?'

'Yep! I'll go down and get the paper and we'll see what's on.'

Fourteen

It was lonely now. Lily wasn't going to stay with Jo as much as she used to. She was glad she'd taken on the petrol station job again so she had the excuse not to stay over. She felt a fool and she couldn't go to Bligh's and pretend that everything was okay. It wasn't and she didn't want to see Tom. A letter arrived from him a week later. He had written:

Dear Lily,

I want you to know that I am truly sorry for what you are going through. I wish you would let me help you. I haven't been able to eat or sleep since I last saw you and I've even had to change jobs as the boys at work were giving me a hard time and were saying I was mooning around like a lovesick girl! I work in Sevenoaks High Street now in a hardware shop. The hours are much easier.

Anyway, Lily, I will keep on writing until you agree to see me. Look after yourself and I look forward to the day you write back to me.

All my love, Tom xxxxx

She cried and resolved not to read his letters after that. What was done was done and she would just have to get on with it as best she could. She knew he was sad but she had too much else to worry about and put it out of her mind. At night she would cry herself to sleep. She couldn't even be bothered to look out of the window at the stars in the sky. No beautiful designs came into her head to make her smile before she went to sleep.

As each day went by she knew it was getting nearer to the time she had to tell her parents. Lily rang the social worker and discussed it with her. She needed to get it over with. She asked if Miss Lindsay thought it would be okay now. She wasn't likely to have a miscarriage now, was she? Miss Lindsay agreed that it wasn't likely.

'You're at the three-month mark now, Lily, and you seem to be a very strong, hearty girl and unlikely to miscarry. I think you'll be okay to tell your parents now. Good luck! Let me know if there's a problem.'

'Thanks, Miss Lindsay. If they throw me out into the street I will ring you.' It was an attempt at humour but neither of them was sure.

Lily waited until she and her mother were alone one afternoon. 'Mum,' she said. 'I need to tell you something.'

Her mother was sitting in her armchair, looking exhausted from her part-time job and all the work of looking after a family of five. She was normally the last to go to bed and the first to rise in the morning. Lily's feelings towards her mother softened. She realised her mum didn't know much about life. She had moved away from her family and friends in Hampshire after the war to be in Kent with her father and she didn't have much of a life at all. She still looked beautiful, tall with dark hair, hazel eyes, a full mouth and remarkably fine skin. Everything was beginning to fade now and the grey hair was showing. She had a large bosom and plump hips and Lily knew that she would have to be careful herself for the rest of her life to keep her own hips and breasts from becoming that large. Ha! Lily caught herself with the ludicrous thought, given that her own hips and breasts were about to become enormous. Her mother turned and looked at her with tired eyes. 'What, Lily? I want to watch *I Love Lucy* and have a rest before I have to go into the kitchen and start making dinner.'

Ignoring her mother's irritable tone, Lily pressed on, saying 'I don't want you to worry because I've got everything planned, but I'm pregnant.'

Her mother's head shot up, shocked out of her apathy. 'Lily! How could you?'

'Look, I was the only girl my age at school not having sex and then I met Tom and he really loved me, Mum. So I thought I would get away with it for a couple of months before I went on the birth control pill.'

Her mother's eyes narrowed. 'I never liked the look of that boy or that friend of yours.'

'Yes, I know that, Mum, but Tom and Jo really cared about me and I enjoyed being with them.' Lily choked on a sob as she made an effort to calm herself. 'I told you I have worked it all out. I went to a doctor in Tonbridge and had it confirmed. He gave me the number of a social worker in Maidstone and she has booked me into an unmarried mothers' home just outside of Maidstone. I will leave school at the end of the year and get a job. I will work until I'm six months and then I can go into the home. After the birth the baby will be adopted. Then you can tell everyone that I got a job in London and they won't know. You and Dad won't be embarrassed, Mum; no-one will have to know.'

Her mother stared at Lily as she took in what she was saying and then looked somewhat appeased by it. Lily had tears in her eyes and got up and gave her mum a rare hug. 'I'm sorry, Mum.' She kept it short as her mother never seemed at ease with shows of affection. 'But, Mum, will you tell Dad when I'm not here? I'm too scared and he won't hit you like he would me. Just tell him everything is organised and no-one will know, okay?'

'All right, Lily.' Her mother abruptly turned from her to put on her TV show. Lily thought she saw a shimmer of a tear in the corner of her eye before she got out of her armchair to press the ON button.

'Mum, I'll go out tonight for a couple of hours. Can you tell him tonight and get it over with?'

'Yes, I'll tell him.' She didn't take her gaze from the TV screen.

'Thanks, Mum.' Lily couldn't wait to leave the room and change her clothes so she could get out of the house before her father came home. As she climbed the stairs her mind went to the time that he came looking for her during last year's summer fair. The fair was something to look forward to. The painted lorries had ambled into the village and set up in a field down the road. They put up the dodgem cars, the Helter Skelter, the Ferris Wheel and many other rides that thrilled her. There was candy floss and hot-dog stands and people laughing and shrieking. Throughout her childhood, along with the Sunday school outing to Folkestone beach, it was the highlight of her year.

At night there were bands and dancing but she always had to be home before dark. Last year they had Acker Bilk playing and Lily loved the music so much she decided to stay and listen. The sound of the clarinet being played with such tenderness made her close her eyes and feel like she was in heaven with the angels.

Bob Roberts, a neighbour, had come up to her and tapped her on the shoulder. With a worried look on his face, he had told her that she had better get home quick as he had seen her dad looking for her. She felt defiant and had shrugged and told him that she didn't care and carried on standing there, listening to the clarinet. Soon after, her brother Simon came rushing up to her and told her that she'd better run home straight away as her father was looking for her and that he was in a rage and he would kill her if he caught her. She had told him that she didn't care and she just wanted to listen to the music.

As soon as Acker Bilk finished she ran as fast as her long legs would take her and hoped she would get into her bed before her father returned home. But he was waiting for her, his face contorted with anger; he took off his leather belt and lashed her several times. She fell to the floor and curled into a ball covering her face with her hands until he stopped. She knew his rage was short-lived and it would subside in a few minutes. The memory made her stomach and neck muscles clench. Feeling sick she hurried so she could get out sooner.

Fifteen

Her parents didn't mention her pregnancy after that and neither did Lily. It was weird but Lily thought she should thank her lucky stars that she didn't have to talk about it. She realised that this was the way they were in life. They didn't talk about anything.

After a few weeks, Lily got very ill. It was late November; the days were damp and foggy, the nights freezing cold. This time, after days in bed, her mother called Dr Ferris. He was a caring man and had tended to Lily since she was a young child. He examined Lily and advised them that she had bronchitis. He asked her mum to step out of the bedroom. The door was left ajar and she heard Dr Ferris ask her mother in hushed tones if she knew that Lily was pregnant. Her mother said she knew and although it was muffled whispers, he raised his voice a little and said, 'But why didn't you bring her to me? Maybe we could have done something about it.'

Lily could detect the frustration in his voice. Straining her ears, she couldn't quite make out her mother's reply, but she knew she would be telling him that her daughter was very headstrong or something to that effect and that she had made up her mind to go into the unmarried mothers' home and have the baby adopted.

He came back into the room and laid his cool hand on her hot, clammy brow and said, 'Look after yourself, Lily. I'll write a prescription and you should feel better in a few days. I want you to know you can come and see me any time.' His eyes looked down into hers, full of kindness and compassion. Lily was feeling delirious but she managed a small smile and a mumble of thanks.

Once he was gone, she turned her face to the wall and tears even hotter than her fever rolled down her flaming cheeks. She wanted it to be over. She felt humiliated by Dr Ferris having to know her secret. It still wasn't real. She didn't seem that much bigger. It got hidden in her 'puppy fat'. After a while she turned over and stared at the ceiling. The same ceiling she had stared at for fifteen years. Had it ever been painted? She wasn't sure. It wasn't dirty, just dull. The walls were painted cream and uninspiring. She'd never really taken the time to look at it before. She had always been aware that because she was the only girl she got the bedroom to herself. It was her haven. She liked her bed and although the room was always cold, with only lino and a round pink mat on the floor, she was warm enough with her hot water bottle, burrowed under the pink feather eiderdown. She decided as soon as she had the energy that she would have to look in the newspapers for a job but for now she just pulled the covers over her face and blotted everything out.

One morning about a week later, Lily was feeling much better and had taken her pillow and eiderdown downstairs so she could lie on the couch and watch TV. It was cold but she could see a pale blue sky and some weak sunshine through the window. She heard the unmistakeable whoosh and plop sound that meant a paper had been shoved through the front door letterbox. She frowned, wondering what day it was. It was Friday and it would be the *Kent Messenger* so she pushed the eiderdown to one side to go and get it. Looking in the job section but not expecting much, she was surprised to find that there were several jobs advertised and one that sounded very interesting. It was one stop away on the train, in Paddock Wood. A plastics factory wanted a receptionist/switchboard operator. She reasoned it would be sitting down and must be easy.

A few days later at the interview she told them she was leaving school in three weeks and liked the sound of the job. She dressed nicely and interviewed well and Mr Busby seemed pleased to give Lily the position.

On her first day she was very nervous. Mr Busby welcomed her and then handed her over to a plump, homely woman called Mrs Wyatt. Mrs Wyatt asked her to sit at the switchboard and Lily was aghast when she saw that it literally was a big board nearly three feet wide and almost as high and each time someone rang you had to put them through to a certain number on the board. Mr Busby, being the owner of the factory, was number one and they went through to twenty-eight. To connect the customer calling to the right person, Lily had to take the lead with a plug on it and plug it into the right hole on the board. Several calls came in whilst Mrs Wyatt was showing her and she would say, 'Shortens Plastics, how can I help you?' Then she deftly took a lead and plugged it into a number on the board and said something like, 'Daphne, a Mr Jones from so-and-so for you.'

'There, dear, do you see how it works?'

Lily nodded her head but she didn't have a clue. She hadn't dreamed it was going to be this difficult.

She was left alone to get on with it. She was fine if a person came into reception and wanted to see someone but as soon as the phone buzzed she had to refer to her list and put a lead into some hole on the board. She would hold her breath and say hesitantly, 'Er, is that Mr Busby?' Or whoever she was hoping it would be. For days it usually wasn't the right person on the other end but they were all good-natured about it and tried to help her out. By the end of the week she was actually enjoying it and rarely made a mistake.

The three months couldn't go fast enough for Lily. Christmas came and went and was the same as every other Christmas, except that Lily hid in her room for longer than ever before. For the first time in her life, she was actually glad that her parents were not sociable people as it meant they had few visitors. January and

February were bitterly cold and there was often snow, ice or sludge on the ground. She had to be extra careful not to slip as she made her way to the station and back each day.

She missed her friends at school and she rarely saw Jo now. She often wondered what Jo was doing at weekends. She seemed as if she was very busy if ever they talked on the phone. She decided to ring Jo as soon as she got home.

'Hello, Mrs Price, could I speak to Joanne, please?'

There was a silence for a moment as if Mrs P was considering whether to let her talk to her daughter, then she said, 'Hold on, Lily, I'll call her, she's in her room. Joanne? Get down here, Lily's on the phone.'

Lily heard the clunk of the Bakelite handpiece being put on the wooden hall table, Jo's bedroom door opening and the thud, thud of footsteps coming down the stairs.

'Hello, Lily?'

'Hello, Jo. I thought I'd give you a call as we haven't spoken much lately. How's school? Are you still going out with the fancy bloke you told me about?'

'I wouldn't call Robert fancy. I see him sometimes, not so much as I did. School is very strenuous now but I'm getting through it. Did you see if you could study part time?'

'I thought about it but I'm so exhausted, I wouldn't be able to do it, especially on my own. I'm not as brainy as you, Jo.'

'Yes, you are, but in a different way, that's all.'

There was an awkward silence. Lily asked, 'Have you seen Tom lately?'

Jo hesitated before she answered. 'He's got a job in a shop in Sevenoaks now so I see him sometimes there or at the pub.'

Lily sensed she didn't want to talk about him but ploughed on with, 'Yes, he wrote to me and said he'd changed his job. I didn't read his other letters so I was hoping he's okay now.'

'He's okay.' After another silence on the line, Jo said, 'I gotta go now, Lily, lots of homework to do. Look after yourself. Talk to you soon.'

'Okay, Jo. Look after yourself too. 'Bye.'

Jo seemed like a stranger now; Lily knew she wouldn't be ringing her again. Not until all this was over anyway. She was getting fewer letters from Tom so she was guessing he'd got the message.

The night before Lily was to go into the unmarried mothers' home finally arrived. She'd left it to the last minute to sew the name labels on her clothes. It was March and there were signs of spring. There were a few sunny days and daffodils and crocuses were coming out everywhere. Lily loved all flowers but her favourites were bluebells and primroses. These grew best out in the woods.

When she was younger she would bike out of the village for miles and go into the woods in springtime just to see and smell the flowers. She'd drop her bike by the grass and walk into the wood. It would be still and gloomy but Lily would eagerly clamber through vines and over dead branches that would crunch and break under her weight making a deafening, cracking sound that would reverberate through the sound of silence. She would keep walking as quietly as possible until she found her prize, a carpet of vibrant and sweet-smelling bluebells. She would sit on a log and become still like the wood itself. If she was lucky she would see rabbits and squirrels and all kinds of little birds, hopping around. She would feel awed that they would accept her there, carrying on as if there was no intruder in their midst. After a while Lily would slowly get up and carefully pick some bluebells and some nearby pale yellow primroses to take home. She'd never felt afraid. It was peaceful like she imagined heaven to be. Once puberty came she couldn't escape on her bike anymore, she would have looked ridiculous. When did the skinny tomboy go and the plump adolescent take her place, she wondered absently.

As she recalled the peace the visits to the woods brought her, she longed for that simplicity to be in her life now. Sitting on the sofa, she bowed her head back to the arduous task of sewing labels onto the hideous maternity clothes. She resented it and didn't see why it was necessary. But she was assured it was a rule. She didn't like sewing but luckily her mum had offered to help and was sitting in her armchair, sewing much more efficiently than Lily ever could. Not that there were many clothes. Lily was six months pregnant now and trying hard to conceal it. Her breasts were a lot bigger and so was her belly. Her mother had managed to find her a couple of dresses in a second-hand shop in Maidstone. When she gave them to Lily she had made sure her father wasn't around and it was a rare collusion between them. Lily was touched that she had looked for clothes for her even though her mother still hadn't said a word about her condition or the upcoming and now imminent departure of her only daughter to an unmarried mothers' home. She had been given a top and a skirt from Miss Lindsay so she now had four outfits but she still had to sew labels on her underwear. Lily thought miserably that it didn't really matter that they're huge and ugly, she'd be stuck away in a home for the next three months and no-one will see her anyway.

A rap-rap of the door knocker made Lily and Mrs Davis look up at each other, startled. People rarely knocked on their front door. 'I'll see who it is, Mum.' She got up and stretched, glad for an excuse to stop sewing. Opening the door, she found a middle-aged man in a suit and a raincoat staring up at her. He looked a caricature of a detective. 'Evening, miss, I'm Detective Barnes from Maidstone Police Station, are you Lily Davis?'

'Yes!' Lily's eyes narrowed suspiciously. 'What do you want?'

'I'm here about the charge of carnal knowledge against Tom Bennett.'

Before he had time to say anything else Lily's eyes flashed angrily. 'I've already told them that I will not press charges; it takes two to tango.' She started to close the door. He was quick to reply, a smug look on his face. 'It's out of your hands now, miss, there are two girls under sixteen that are pregnant by him.'

Lily held onto the door. She felt as if she'd been punched and winded. She instantly knew who the other girl was. 'Is the other girl's name Joanne Price?'

'Yes, that's right, miss. We will need you to attend the court case in a month's time. Here's the summons. We'll see you all in court.'

Lily shut the door on the officious bastard and went back into the lounge room. Her mother was looking at her inquisitively. 'Who was that, Lily?'

Lily explained, clenching her jaw. Her mother tsked and said for the hundredth time how she had never trusted that Joanne anyway. Lily thought about explaining how she was the bad one for taking away the boy that Jo loved but she felt overwhelmed and she couldn't talk about it. 'He loved me, Mum, and I don't want him prosecuted. I don't want to go.'

She sat down heavily in her chair and threw the sewing aside. She couldn't be bothered to do anymore. With a shrug of her shoulders she wondered what could they do to her anyway. Her mother, used to having to stay quiet for years, didn't say anymore. They were both glad that Lily's father was at his gardening club. Bill Davis also had a love of flowers. He was happiest in his garden and grew burgundy red dahlias, huge white chrysanthemums and a wonderful assortment of roses. He won prizes most years. He also had a very large allotment near his sister Mary's house and worked every weekend and some evenings, digging the soil and planting carrots, cabbages, beetroot, onions, beans, even potatoes, giving them a constant supply of fresh vegetables.

When Lily was small, she sometimes helped him on a Sunday morning. She was fascinated by the huge pink worms he would dig up. They were often more than six inches long and as thick as a finger. He would hold them up, wriggling between his finger and thumb to show her, and laugh as she screamed and ran away. Lily knew her father worked very hard. She also knew he had a very gentle side that she would see only when he was with his plants.

'Mum, thanks for helping me with this and for everything. Don't worry, it will all sort itself out. He asked me to marry him and I told him to get lost so I can't blame him for what he does now. Miss Lindsay will be here at ten o'clock to take me to the home. You'll be at work so let's say goodbye now.'

'I won't see you for a while, Lily, so I will come and say goodbye tomorrow before I leave, all right?'

'All right, Mum, I'd like that. Goodnight.' She gave her mother another quick hug, gathered up her clothes and as quickly as she was able, went up the stairs to her room. Unable to hold herself together a moment longer, Lily collapsed on top of her bed, crying tears of desperation. No matter what she had said to her mother she felt betrayed as if she had been stabbed repeatedly in the back, by both Jo and Tom. It seemed they had they forgotten about her and she was out of sight out of mind. She cried until she fell asleep, still with her clothes on.

Sixteen

Waking up cold and uncomfortable at some ungodly hour, still lying on top of her bed, Lily crawled under the covers. Now wide awake, she couldn't get back to sleep and wanted to scream out loud and not stop screaming until she woke up from this nightmare. She waited until all the family had left except her mother, before she ventured out to the bathroom.

Her mother came in and sat on her bed; she paused as if she didn't know what to say then awkwardly bent forward giving her a peck on the cheek and a half hug, saying, 'Goodbye, Lily. Look after yourself.' Then just as quickly, she was gone, shutting the bedroom door behind her. Sadness engulfed Lily as she keenly felt her mother's absence and wondered when she would see her again. She threw the covers aside and distracted herself by getting ready. Once dressed and unable to eat, she waited anxiously, looking out of the lounge room window.

She wanted to get to wherever she was going quickly, as if by doing so it would speed up the long, drawn-out process of having a baby.

She watched as a pale blue Corsair come to a halt in the cul-de-sac. Gathering up her jacket and the small case, she made her way to the front door and opened it before Miss Lindsay had a chance to knock. Saying 'hello', they walked to the car. Lily, feeling resigned to her fate, awkwardly got in, onto the low front seat. She wanted to hide as they drove up the road, past the neighbours' houses. She felt people were peering at her behind their white net curtains and knew where she was being taken. Shrinking back in her seat, she felt shame and misery.

Soon they were out of Highden and driving along the narrow, winding roads, bypassing Maidstone until they were in the countryside in an area that Lily didn't know. Miss Lindsay turned the car into a long and wide gravel driveway. Lily saw manicured grass and lots of shrubs and trees either side. As they got closer she could see that the home was an old, imposing two-storey mansion with greyish-white paint flaking off the walls. It had a sinister feel and Lily felt a sense of foreboding. Getting out of the car, the feeling grew as a tall, upright, middle-aged woman with short dark hair came down the steps to meet them. 'Ah! Miss Lindsay, this must be Lily Davis.'

It was a statement not a question and her small brown eyes, set back under thick brown eyebrows, bored into Lily's. The expression on her pale, hard face conveyed disdain as though Lily was another cheap girl here to pay for her sins. She was relieved that Miss Lindsay stayed cheerful, saying, 'Yes, that's right, Miss Simms. I'll just bring her case up and make sure she's settled in her room.'

'There's no need for that, Miss Lindsay, the girl can carry it herself; she's not an invalid.'

'I insist, Miss Simms; she is in my care until I see her into the premises.'

Wow! Lily thought, Miss Lindsay may be young but she's no pushover. Miss Simms looked like a right old battle-axe.

As they walked up the wide circular steps and in through the heavy oak door, the leadlight panels either side of the door flashed vibrant reds and blues in the sunshine, a sharp contrast to the gloom inside. Lily looked around and saw that the entrance hall was wide and had oak floorboards. There was a magnificent sweeping staircase going up the centre and then around to the left and the right, distracting Lily for a moment as she thought of Scarlett O'Hara in *Gone with the Wind*. As she studied her new surroundings, Lily noticed a heavily pregnant girl, on her hands and knees, polishing the floorboards above them. Shock zipped through her as she wondered what on earth was going on. Miss Lindsay had a closed look on her face and Miss Simms was talking in her clipped tone, oblivious to how incongruous it looked.

With a wave of her hand, Miss Simms indicated for them to go up the highly polished stairs with a worn maroon carpet. How many girls have gone up and down these stairs, Lily wondered.

'You will have duties, Miss Davis, like all the girls, from nine a.m. until twelve noon. I like to keep the place ship-shape and it stops the girls from having idle hands.' Miss Simms looked round at Miss Lindsay with a satisfied look on her face as she said this, as if to indicate in a conspirative way that she knew what was best for these wayward girls. Lily was horrified, thinking, what have I come to. This looks like something out of Dickens. She felt very nervous. They climbed to the top of the stairs and forked off to the right, hurrying to keep up with the brisk pace of Miss Simms. She opened a door at the end of the hallway with a flourish and sailed through it, Miss Lindsay and Lily trailing in her wake.

The room was square with lots of light; there were four single beds made up. Miss Simms turned to Lily. 'This is your bed for the duration of your stay, Miss Davis.'

Lily's heart sank again. She wasn't sure how she'd cope with sharing a room with three strangers. Biting her lip, she decided she would cope no matter what. 'Thank you.' It was all she could manage.

'Will you be all right, Lily?' Miss Lindsay had a concerned look on her face. 'Here's my card. You can ring me at any time if you need me.' She pressed the card into her hand looking straight into Lily's eyes.

'I'll see you out, Miss Lindsay,' Miss Simms said crisply, taking back control again. She turned to Lily. 'Unpack your case, Miss Davis, into the cupboard beside the bed. Put the case under the bed ready for the day you're taken to the hospital. Come down to my office when you're finished.' Miss Simms left the room as determinedly as she had entered it with Miss Lindsay close behind her.

Lily sat heavily on the bed. She hadn't known what to expect but it wasn't anything like this. Tears filled her eyes and she hastily wiped them away with her hand. Misery was threatening to engulf her but she couldn't give into that now. Looking out of the window she was cheered by the sight of towering trees with fresh, new green leaves. She stood up so that she could look down into the rest of the garden below. She could see beautiful rhododendron bushes flowering with big pink blooms and some bright yellow daffodils. The first month of spring was normally a time when Lily rejoiced. This was the sign that winter had lost its depressing grey hold on the English countryside. The view cheered Lily enough to get up off the bed and unpack her meagre supply of clothes. Then taking a deep breath, she straightened her shoulders and walked determinedly out of the room and down the stairs.

Seventeen

Lily could see an oak panelled door that was closed, to the right of the bottom of the stairs. As she approached, seeing the name on the plaque was indeed Miss Simms, she knocked softly. A voice boomed, 'Enter'.

Walking into the office hesitantly, she looked over at Miss Simms sitting behind an enormous desk. 'Shut the door, Lily.'

Lily shut the sturdy door and turned expectantly.

'Now I will tell you the rules of this establishment only once. It is up to you to do what is required of you and strictly adhere to these rules. First of all, you will at all times behave in an orderly and ladylike manner. You will not raise your voice and you will be on time for all meals and your duties. I will give you a timetable for the meals and a roster for your duties. Your duty will be in the laundry and you will be doing the ironing for the household. You will start at nine a.m. and finish at twelve noon, Monday to Friday. Any questions?'

Lily was too stunned to ask a question. By now she was in her seventh month of pregnancy and had thought she would be left pretty much to herself to get through it until the birth. She felt stunned that the girls were expected to clean this big, old place. She couldn't believe it. Thoughts raced through her mind. She noticed Miss Simms looking at her with an eyebrow raised and realised she had better say something. 'No, Miss Simms.'

'Good! Then we understand each other. I run a tight ship here and bad behaviour will not be tolerated. If you have a problem, then come and see me. Here are your timetable and roster. You will start tomorrow morning. Lateness will not be acceptable for meals or for duties. That's all, Miss Davis; you may go to your room now until you hear the bell for lunch. The dining room is to the left of the stairs. After lunch I will show you the laundry and the library. The bathrooms are down the hall to the right of your room.' She got up from behind her desk abruptly and Lily felt momentarily afraid.

'Thank you, Miss Simms.' She turned and almost ran out of the room, being careful to shut the door quietly behind her. She managed to hold it together until she was back up the stairs and into her allotted bedroom. She hastily looked around her and seeing there was no one else in the room, threw herself on the bed and cried as quietly as she could. She felt angry and frustrated and more alone than ever before. Misery pressed like a weight on her heart. Lily took in a gulp of air and then froze when she heard the doorknob turn. She shot upright and scrabbled for her hanky up her sleeve and wiped her eyes. A plump, plain-faced girl looked over at her whilst closing the door. She looked friendly, Lily thought, as she blew her nose noisily.

'I'm Catherine,' the girl said quietly.

'I'm Lily. I just arrived.'

'You'll get used to it, don't worry. It's a terrible shock when you first arrive. Not what you'd expect. The girls are mainly nice. We help each other get through it.'

There was something comforting in the sturdy girl's manner. 'This is my bed here.' She walked around and sat on the bed across from Lily's.

Lily blew her nose some more and felt the solidarity of someone nice to share the nightmare with. 'Why are we expected to do all the cleaning and ironing around here? Wouldn't the government pay people to do that?'

'We think they probably do but the old bat pockets that money and makes us do it to punish us.'

'That looks about right. What chores do you do?'

'I have to clean the bedrooms. There are two of us and we do four of the eight rooms each. Each room has four girls and the place is full. I'm due in six weeks and once I go into hospital there'll be someone to take my place the same day.'

'Oh!' Lily felt shocked, now seeing the stark reality of so many of them needing a place to go. She felt wobbly again but managed to ask through some tears that escaped and slid down her cheeks, 'What are you going do with your baby?'

Their eyes locked in mutual misery and Catherine's were watery as she said, 'I want to marry Dave; I love him and he loves me and we have been going out for nearly two years but my parents won't let us. They said that we're too young. They are forcing me to have my baby adopted but we want to keep it and get married.' She was trying hard not to cry. 'They'll take the baby after three days and then I have to go back home and they say I'm not allowed to see Dave anymore.'

'Catherine, that's awful. If you love each other and you both want the baby, why won't they let you?'

'They're religious for one thing and they don't want to be embarrassed with their friends and neighbours. That's all they seem to care about. They don't care about my feelings at all.'

Tears rolled down Catherine's cheeks and Lily could tell that the girl was tired to the bone and probably sick of telling her story for the hundredth time. 'I'm scared I'm not strong enough to get through this.' Catherine looked into Lily's eyes again.

Lily understood as she was feeling terrified. 'It's a horrendous situation to be in. I'm scared too but I'm also angry and frustrated that I'm in this place instead of being at school studying for my A levels.'

'What are you going to do then?'

'I'm going to have the baby adopted after three days also. Then my friend and I were going to get a flat in Paris and work there for a few years. Except that I found out yesterday that she's just got pregnant as well. It hasn't sunk in yet. I don't know what she's going to do now.'

Lily felt like someone had thrown cold water over her as she realized she had been so angry with Tom and Jo that she hadn't thought it through as to how it was going to affect her and Jo's long-term plans. Jo would be having her baby months after her and everything would be delayed. Her heart felt as though it was sinking into a pit of renewed despair. She looked at Catherine and realised she didn't feel like talking about this anymore. The bell went and they both stood up.

'I'll show you where the dining room is, come on.'

As they walked out a couple of girls rushed in. They stopped in their tracks when they saw a new girl standing there. 'Susan, Leah, this is Lily. She arrived this morning.'

'Hi Lily!' they said. 'Give us two secs and we'll be right behind you.'

Lily allowed herself to be ushered along into the dining room by the girls. They all seemed okay and she thought that maybe it wouldn't be so bad sharing a room after all.

Eighteen

At six-thirty the loud, insistent bell drilled into Lily's ears, jolting her into consciousness. Her roommates stirred and muttered, resenting such a rude awakening every morning. Knowing the bell would go a full minute before stopping, no-one said a word, they'd exhausted all avenues of bitching about Miss Simms' ploys to make their lives a misery.

'Come on, let's get going,' said Leah, who was the most active of the four of them and cheerfully organised them at every opportunity. They dragged themselves out of bed without delay, knowing that getting to the bathroom before the other girls along the hallway meant they'd have time to sit and chat before breakfast. Lily found the distraction of sharing her plight with her roommates was better than keeping her misery and bewilderment to herself. She still got her much-needed time to herself when in the laundry but she looked forward to their talks. Enjoying this time to be idle, they never tired of chatting and by the time they had got washed and dressed they were awake enough to sit on their beds and talk about all the things they had done and all the things they wanted to do.

The bell started up again, summoning them down for breakfast. They jumped up, as much as their condition would allow, and looked at each other with the unspoken agreement that they would continue their talk at bedtime. They went down the stairs slowly as Catherine was extremely large now. They eyed her all the time, watching for signs of labour.

Breakfast was tea and white toast. They had eggs on Sundays. Lily worried about how the awful food could sustain them let alone sustain another being growing inside them. The dining room was hushed, it wasn't worth risking Miss Simms' wrath, so they ate in silence until it was time for them to file out. The drill was that they would clean their teeth, go to the toilet and then do the mandatory two rounds of the manicured back garden that was as large as a cricket pitch. Then it was time to begin their chores. Lily was numb from the oppression and the dull and arduous routine. She never dreamed it would be like this or that the time would go so interminably.

Alone down in the basement in the big laundry with its industrial washing machine, Lily began the ironing for the day. She didn't really mind, it was the best job for her, being quiet down there and no-one else around. Although she welcomed the time to think, with her predisposition to depression, she knew she had to be careful not to think about everything too much. If she wasn't vigilant it could take a hold of her and throw her down a deep, dark hole. Once down there it was almost impossible to scrabble up and out of it again.

On autopilot, she went over and over different scenarios of how Jo and Tom got together. Remembering clearly how Jo had once said that she went to see Tom sometimes after school to let him know how Lily was getting on. Lily hardened her heart again towards Jo, knowing this was just a ruse to see Tom. Now he worked in the High street it was easy for Jo to just pop in. Lily extrapolated that after a few visits that would probably have become, did he want to go to the pub for a drink after he finished work. Tom would have said something like, yeah, okay then. That would have led on to commiserations and probably getting drunk together and somewhere along the line, it would have led to sex. Lily was getting herself in a state and felt more angry and alone than ever, furiously using the extra energy to iron the pillow cases and sheets.

Her right hand now had calluses across the palm but she was too weary to be indignant about it anymore. Lily had watched her mother iron for hours when she was young and accepted it as a necessary part of life. Her thoughts drifted back to how mean and meagre the food was and decided it was probably another rort by Miss Simms or at the very least, another way she could make their lives intolerable. She realised that all the home-cooked meals that her mum had made had probably given her all the goodness that she had needed; tears sprang into her eyes as if they'd been on starting blocks and someone had shot the gun. She felt like a small child again at the thought of her mother. In the six weeks she'd been here no-one had come to see her and she missed her mum more than she would have thought possible. Her parents would get a shock at how enormous she looked now. With resignation, she knew her dad wouldn't allow her mother to come and visit. He didn't allow anything, really.

Lily smiled as an image leapt into her mind of her mother spontaneously jumping up from her armchair and doing an Irish jig to the music from some band on TV. Her father would always tell her not to be so bloody silly and to sit down. Her mother, used to it, would laugh and then sit down again. Lily wondered how on earth she managed to keep her spirits up after all those years. Her smile faded quickly. Her mother never got any praise for all her efforts of cooking good meals for the five of them every night. Lily daydreamed of the steak-and-kidney pies with piles of fresh vegetables and mashed potatoes, or the Hungarian goulash with dumplings. Then there would be apple pie and custard or rice pudding. Her mouth was watering. As she pictured her family sitting around the table, the reality quickly spoiled the fantasy. Being here was not that much worse than the family all tiptoeing around her father, never knowing when he may lash out. Her thoughts brought fresh guilt; she'd never thanked her mum much either. Tears hovered again as she acknowledged how much she appreciated it now. Suddenly, her anger flared. Neither her mother nor her father had ever taken the time to ask how she was getting on at school, ever. Again, she thought that she might not be in this bloody mess if they had taken more of an interest in her.

She thought she'd done well, considering everything. At eleven she had passed the eleven-plus exam but had to make her own decision as to what school she would go to for her secondary education. Suddenly, like going through a time warp in the TARDIS, she saw herself sitting in the dark and cluttered headmaster's office. She had felt small and alone, not knowing what to expect and looking at three teachers seated in a row, staring back at her. An old grandfather clock had ticked noisily and the smell of the dusty burgundy Persian carpet had assaulted her nose. They could have been back in the 1890s when the school was built.

Mrs Carroll had told her that she had passed the eleven-plus exam well. She'd jumped as she'd been spoken to but then had been aware of a pause. Lily had known this was good news and thought she should feel pleased but she had been able to tell that there was a 'but' coming. Then the headmaster had said that they wondered what she wanted to do as a career. She had confessed she didn't know. He went on to ask her if her parents had discussed it with her and had then enquired why her parents weren't there with her. They hadn't known that in her case it was a stupid question. She remembered it clearly as if it was last week and could still feel the shame of being a kid whose parents didn't care enough to be there on such an important day. After she told them her parents were both at work they had asked if she had thought about what career she may like to study for, adding that this would help them best guide her to the most appropriate school she had qualified for. Her mind had searched wildly for an answer. She had reasoned that she liked cutting and setting her mother's hair; she was good at that so she had told them that she could be a hairdresser. Their quick retort was that she was too clever for that. She had felt like she was being admonished rather than praised. But she did enjoy doing hair; it was creative and made her feel useful.

Mrs Carroll had advised that she had passed with high enough marks that she had the choice of Tonbridge Grammar School or the Tonbridge Girls' Technical School. She had longed for her mother to be there to guide her but had to think quickly what to do. The Grammar school sounded too grand for her and she had picked up that the Technical school was for girls only, so she decided on the Girls' Tech. No boys, less aggravation. There had been an awkward silence where she had seen the headmaster and the teachers look at each other before they told her that they would put her down for the Technical school. They had wished her well and she was then dismissed. Lily wondered how different her life might have been with a different choice. She shrugged her shoulders and looked at the electric clock on the wall behind her. It was five to twelve so she could turn the iron off now and go up for lunch.

Catherine, Susan and Leah were already seated at their allotted table. Lily may have been feeling she was as big as a house but now looking across at Catherine, she realised she still had a way to go. Poor Catherine was due any day. She looked wretched and had dark circles under her eyes. A friend had come in to see her last week and had secretly brought in a letter from her boyfriend Dave. He still loved her but Catherine cried for days. She desperately wanted to keep her baby and was heartbroken that it would be taken away from her. Lily gave her shoulder a squeeze before she sat down. They were all going through hell in one way or another. She gave her a smile and Catherine did her best to smile back but her eyes stayed dull. At least I don't have the agony of being in love with my baby's father and wanting to keep it, Lily thought. She felt sure that she was doing the right thing and that her baby will have good parents. The reminder of her betrayal by the two people she thought loved her swiftly followed and she didn't feel that there was any consolation to be had at all. Her mood darkened and the light went out of Lily's eyes too. Trying to lighten up again, Lily said, 'Who wants to come for a walk after lunch? Summer's nearly here and it's warmer today. It'll do us good.'

Leah, who had been very quiet said, 'I have a headache, Lily. Sorry, I just want to lie down after lunch.'

Susan would always do what Leah did. Catherine looked across at Lily and said in a quiet voice, 'I'll come with you.'

Lily knew she was only trying to please her. Never mind, she decided that it will do her good to get out. Looking around at some of the other girls as they filed out, each one looked weighed down by the reality of what their life had become. Lunch had been corned beef sandwiches with white bread, possibly a bit more tasty than usual but nothing to get excited about. Lily didn't really talk to anyone much outside of their group, but there was the unspoken feeling that they were all sharing the same plight. She looked up as Susan and Leah started up the stairs. 'See you soon. Hope your headache goes.'

As they went through the grand front door, out into the brittle sunshine, it felt like they were going to escape and make a run for it. Lily smiled at the absurdity of them running anywhere and told Catherine why she was smiling. A smile played across Catherine's eyes in acknowledgement. They walked at a leisurely pace down the driveway, crunching along on the gravel in companionable silence. Spring flowers were in full bloom: sweet smelling freesias and a few late dark yellow daffodils. The rose bushes along the driveway were sprouting fresh bright green leaves, ready to take centre stage in summer.

Catherine gasped suddenly and Lily snapped her head around to look at her. 'Lily! My water has just broken!' Catherine's eyes were as round as saucers.

Lily knew implicitly that it wasn't the impending birth that frightened her but that the time had come when she would have to give her baby away. They both looked at the water running down Catherine's legs and then at each other, mirroring each other's fear. Lily put her arm around her, gently turning her back around. 'Can you walk back or do you want me to run and get someone?'

Neither of them knew what was best so Lily told her to stay there and she ran, as much as she was able, and rushed boldly into the office and told Miss Simms.

'Go back and stay with her, Lily.' She looked flustered as if this was putting her out. 'I'll go and find Mrs Smith and tell her to get the car out and run her to the hospital.'

Lily was back out the door as soon as Miss Simms had finished talking and hurried back down the long driveway, shouting, 'Hang on, Catherine, I'm coming.'

Catherine was crying softly and still standing in the pool of water. They could hear the car coming down the drive before it came into view. Mrs Smith wrenched the handbrake on noisily. Jumping out, she questioned Catherine urgently. 'I grabbed your bag, Catherine. How are you feeling? Are there any contractions? Do you feel you would be better in an ambulance?'

Catherine shook her head. She was bundled carefully into the back of the car and they sped off, the tyres hurling gravel everywhere. Catherine's head was turned, her eyes looking desperately into Lily's until she was out of sight. That look haunted Lily for days. She imagined it was the look of someone going to the gallows. Poor Catherine, Lily thought; it would be terrible to have your baby taken from you against your will. She sent up a silent prayer. She would miss her as she had become a friend. Lily made her way miserably up the driveway. She would have to tell Susan and Leah. Who's going to be next, she thought.

Nineteen

One Saturday afternoon in late May, Mrs Smith came bustling into the common room, her eyes darting around the room until they settled on Lily, slumped in a big, old armchair. Lily was settled in to the rare luxury of being allowed to do nothing but watch TV. She was surprised to find this small bird-like woman was actually seeking her out and then was even more surprised to be told she had a visitor. She'd only had two visitors in three months: once when her elder brother, Simon, brought her mother to see her and another time when he brought Sam, her younger brother.

Lily had got used to not hearing her name called at weekends when the other girls had their visitors. It was par for the course with her parents. She had no interest in seeing her father anyway, especially looking like this. She felt as big as a hippopotamus. Her breasts and belly were huge and she weighed in at over twelve stone. She didn't want to see anyone until she looked and felt normal again. Even so, Lily had been pleased that her mother had either gone against her father's wishes or had snuck out without saying where she was going, to come and see her.

She heaved herself out of the chair and followed Mrs Smith down the hall to the visitors' lounge, her mind searching for an answer as to who would be coming to see her. As she entered the room, she saw Jo standing over by the window. 'Jo! What a surprise! How are you? How did you get here?' She walked over to give her a hug. Jo was never effusive but Lily let her go and stood back, feeling her cool reserve.

'I got my brother to drive me. How are you doing, Lily?'

'Not so good. I wrote to you a few times but there's nothing much to say without getting you depressed too. What about you? Are you going to keep your baby?' As Lily searched her friend's face she tried to read the emotions that flitted over it. One looked like 'the cat that got the cream', the next a look of determination.

'I'm going to keep it. And I'm going to marry Tom!'

There, just for a second, was the 'cat that got the cream' look but then Jo's eyes became steely. Disbelief then a surge of anger passed through Lily. For them to have sex was one thing but for Tom to stop loving her so easily and replace her with another in just a few months was devastating. She honestly thought he still loved her. Fury rose up in Lily and it took all her might to hold down the urge to punch Jo hard in the belly making her abort right there on the spot. It felt so real that she looked down, expecting to see the floor covered with blood. Not seeing any, Lily looked up to see Jo's face was impassive. Lily realised her hands were still clenched by her sides and Jo was waiting for a response. 'Oh!' It was hard to speak. 'When is it due?'

'Early November.'

There didn't seem anything left to say. Looking at Jo, Lily noted that she was still looking trim although there was roundness in place of her usual taut stomach. She was nicely dressed in navy-blue linen pants and a white cotton-knit jumper. Her face looked tired though and there were dark circles under her eyes that had never been there before. The bond of friendship between them had gone. Feeling defeated, Lily said, 'Okay, Jo, well, I'm not feeling too good, I'm due in two weeks and I need to go and lie down now. Thanks for coming to tell me.' She started to walk to the door and then turned saying, 'They wanted me to go to court but I got Miss Lindsay to say I was unwell. What happened? Did Tom have to go to prison?'

'No. They said because he was eighteen and neither of us wanted to prosecute that they would let him off with a warning.'

'That's all right then. Goodbye, Jo.' Lily turned and with as much dignity as she could find, she straightened her back and walked out of the room.

Twenty

Lily didn't know how she was going to get back to her room without screaming. Pushing her hand tightly to her mouth she hauled herself up the long length of stairs. Sobs burst through as she opened the door to her room, her eyes swiftly seeing that it was empty. Thanking God, she kicked the door shut and fell on her bed. She kept thinking: How could he? How could he? Choking, she realised she wasn't thinking it, she was screaming it out loud. She felt she would die if anyone came in. She clamped her hand back over her mouth but sobs were racking her body. A dam of emotion broke free, allowing memories, emotions and pictures to surface from deep down inside.

Now the dam had burst, nothing could hold it back. The pain of being abandoned again was like a knife cutting her in two. The sheer effort of pushing down the overwhelming urge to scream at the top of her lungs suddenly made her feel exhausted with the futility of it all. Her thoughts slowed and she felt pure anger: anger at Tom, at Jo, at her parents, at God and at herself. It kept building as the stifled emotions pushing against the dam had done. Feeling energised by her mounting fury, she pushed herself up off the bed.

Catching sight of herself in the mirror, shock and loathing made her want to throw a heavy object and smash the ugly image. Her face was red and bloated, her hair standing on end. Her body looked like a huge, pale-blue Crimplene blimp! Her own clothes hadn't fitted her for weeks and she was given clothes donated by 'do-gooders'. They were all 'fifties' in their style: ugly and drab. Lily hated the Crimplene maternity top with its tiny bow on the small collar and the pleats that fell over her swollen body. She wore it because it was the only thing that fitted and she didn't think anyone would be seeing it anyway. Now it was like seeing herself for the first time. How utterly ugly she looked. She wanted to tear her hideous clothes off and throw them out the open window; she wanted her body and face to shrink back to their normal proportions. Looking at her reflection staring back at her, she knew none of this was going to happen. The energy moving through her felt malevolent and wanted to lash out. As if driven by a demon, she rushed to find her scissors and hacked at her hair, pulling it out and chopping it off, giving her great satisfaction to be able to do harm to something. The frenzy subsided and looking again at her reflection, her hair was now tufts. It didn't matter, nothing did. She'd been a fool just like all his other conquests. She felt damn sure that if you loved someone, it didn't disappear at the drop of a hat. She was no expert but she was a fiercely loyal person and she knew she still loved Jo and always would, no matter what.

Slumping back on the bed, Lily felt strangely calm. Deep down she had been able to draw some comfort that the father of her child loved her. That sliver of comfort was gone now and she was back to there being only one person in her life that she could count on: herself. She felt clearly that after today things could not go on in the same way. Her rage had smashed through the depression and complacency and she knew she could not stay in this place for another minute. She asked herself why had she struggled in this dreadful place for so long. Lowering herself slowly to her knees, she searched through her things for Miss Lindsay's card. Miss Lindsay had come to see her a few times but Lily had never bothered to ring her. What's the use, she would say to herself if ever she felt the inclination to make a change. But Miss Lindsay had told her that if she wasn't happy in the home, she might be able to get her in somewhere else. Now with a burning desire for that to happen, she clutched the card in her sweating hand and walked towards the door. Catching sight of herself in the mirror again, she knew the bathroom would have to be the first stop.

After splashing cold water over her red, swollen eyes and face, she dampened the tufts of hair, trying to smooth them down. Seeing no change, she impatiently walked as fast as she could to the phone, down the stairs in the hallway. Knowing it was Saturday, she wondered what the chances were of getting Miss Lindsay today. Her face began to wobble again and a tear slid out of each eye and ran down her face, blurring her vision so she could barely see the numbers on the dial. Miraculously, the disdainful voice of Miss Greaves came on the line.

'Maidstone Social Services.'

'Hello, it's Lily Davis here.' She faltered and swallowed a sob, knowing she had to calm herself. 'I need to talk to Miss Lindsay, it … it's an emergency.'

She heard Miss Greaves draw in a breath; if she put her off-side she would not get a message through to Miss Lindsay until Monday. By then she would have killed herself. She waited. The silence on the other end seemed interminable.

'What sort of an emergency, miss?'

'I want to kill myself.'

'I see. Well, you're in luck, Miss Davis, Miss Lindsay is just packing up for the weekend and is still in her office. Hold the line please.'

Lily held her breath. Could this be true? Could she be lucky enough that by some fluke, the kind Miss Lindsay was really there?

'Hello! Lily?'

'Hello, Miss Lindsay,' she said, holding back a sob. 'Jo came to see me and she's going to keep her baby and marry Tom and I want to kill myself!' Struggling to control her tears, Lily rushed on. 'Will you please find another home for me? I can't bear to stay in this terrible place another minute.' The sob escaped. 'Please, Miss Lindsay, please.'

'Lily! I want you to take a deep breath and try and calm yourself. I can tell you've had a nasty shock. I have to make a phone call but I'm sure they still have a vacancy in Tunbridge Wells. Stay near the phone and I will call back in five minutes. Do you hear me, Lily?'

There was obvious concern and kindness in Miss Lindsay's voice. Lily felt comforted as she knew she could trust Miss Lindsay to do her best.

Putting the phone back in its cradle she was dimly aware that some of the girls were walking by and looking at her with sympathy. She brushed the tears away and searched for a hanky to blow her nose, embarrassed as snot was running freely from it. Not finding one, she made a frantic dash for the toilet. Seeing the toilets brought on a desperate need to pee. Barging in and slamming the door she became anxious she may miss her phone call. With liquid streaming out of nearly every orifice, she listened intently for the ring as she kept pulling off toilet paper, blowing her nose and wiping her eyes. Suddenly hearing the phone, she struggled to pull her pants up and tug her clothes down. She rushed out to answer it. 'Hello? Lily Davis here.'

'It's Miss Lindsay. I have some good news. They have agreed to take you and you can go right away. Pack your case, Lily. I will phone Miss Simms and I will leave the office soon after. I should be there to pick you up within half an hour. Okay? Lily?'

Lily was unable to believe her good fortune. She felt she needed to pinch herself to make sure it was real.

'Lily?'

'Yes! Yes! Miss Lindsay. I'll be ready. Thank you! Thank you! I don't know what to say.' Tears were pricking her eyes again as they often did when someone showed her kindness.

'You don't have to say anything. Now get off the phone and get yourself ready.'

Feeling like a ten-year-old, 'Yes, Miss!' was all she could manage.

Excitement raced through her. She really was going to escape from this prison, right now, today; she wanted to run up the stairs full pelt but resigned herself to climbing them slowly. She had plenty of time to pack her small collection of things. As she got to the dormitory door she had a sudden pang of sadness to be leaving the girls. It felt like she was deserting them. The truth was, she reminded herself, they would all be leaving soon, one by one, to face their fate. Catherine had already been gone five weeks. She turned the knob and went in and found Katrina and Leah standing by the mirror, talking. They looked up, their faces filled with concern. 'Lily! Are you all right?'

She sank heavily down onto her bed and looked up at them. 'Not really. I've had some awful news and I feel sick and I just want to get out of here.'

'We saw the hair on the floor. We were worried. We knew something had happened. Why did you cut off your hair?' said Katrina, seemingly mesmerised and unable to stop staring at Lily's head.

'I had so much anger surging through me. Hacking my hair off was probably the least damage I could do.'

'You poor thing! Do you want to talk about it?'

'I really don't. I'll just break down all over again. I phoned my social worker and she's found a place in a home in Tunbridge Wells for me. She's coming to get me in about half an hour.'

They both gasped at the speed of her imminent departure. 'What did Miss Simms say? She's not going to like it.'

Lily came down to earth with a thud. She had forgotten she would need to have one last encounter with the mean-spirited Miss Simms. They looked at one another as they realised at the same time that Miss Simms might come thundering in at any minute.

'The hair!' Leah said with alarm. 'We have to clean up the hair!'

They stood up in unison, Lily enormous and cumbersome, Leah, small but very round, and Katrina tall and skinny with a swollen belly sticking out from her frame.

'I'll go and get a dustpan and brush,' said Katrina.

'I'll find a bag of some sort to put it in,' said Leah, already searching for something that would do the job.

'I'll scrape it up into a pile,' Lily said, again getting down on her hands and knees. She looked up at them. 'Thanks! I'll miss you.'

Leah found an old potato crisp bag and held it open as Lily started to put the hair in it. Most of it was in by the time Katrina got back with the dustpan and brush.

'Lily, Leah, quick! Miss Simms is on her way up the stairs!'

They scrambled to their feet. Leah stuffed the bag under a pillow and Katrina shoved the dustpan under a bed. Miss Simms barged through the door, visibly fuming. She stopped when she saw them all standing there. 'What are you all doing in here? Miss Darren, Miss Hartnet, out now!'

Lily saw them squirm under Miss Simms' glare and they left quickly, looking up at Lily through their lashes. Lily sensed their sorrow at having to leave her to it.

She braced herself. Looking straight at Miss Simms, she had to fight an impulse to giggle. Miss Simms looked like something out of a comic book: her eyes were bulging and she looked as though she should have steam coming out of her ears. 'Miss Davis!' she boomed.

Lily didn't feel like giggling anymore.

'I hear from Miss Lindsay that you have gone behind my back and told her you want to leave this establishment.'

Lily could feel her fury. She was glad she was leaving and would not have to endure this place any longer. She said nothing. She had not been asked a question.

'Well, what do you have to say for yourself?'

'I've had some awful news and I'm not happy here. I need to get away or I'll die.'

'Nonsense! You're being unduly melodramatic. You only have another two weeks to go, Miss Davis. Whatever it is, what difference can it make where you are? How am

I going to explain to the board that one of my charges is leaving in this manner?'

'If you didn't put us girls through such misery maybe we wouldn't be in this situation!' Lily angrily retorted.

'I don't know what you mean. This is preposterous. I demand that you reconsider and tell Miss Lindsay that you will stay here until it is your time to leave.'

'No! Miss Simms! I will not reconsider and I will be leaving here in half an hour to go to a home that I have heard actually treats the girls well.' Lily turned and began putting things into her suitcase. She could sense Miss Simms blustering behind her but they both knew there was nothing she could do.

'Well I never!' Miss Simms turned and walked out.

Lily smiled. A small victory but it felt good.

Twenty-one

Hearing a light tap at the door and opening it, Lily was relieved to see Miss Lindsay standing there. She thought she had never been so glad to see someone. 'I feel like you've saved my life.'

'It was pure luck, Lily. Fortunately, I had to go back to the office late this afternoon. I nearly put it off. Now, let's get you out of here before there's any more drama.'

She picked up Lily's case and was ushering her out of the door as if she couldn't bear to be in this awful place a moment longer either. Within minutes they were down the stairs and out the front door, eager to get in the car with the doors firmly closed. Lily looked up at the bedroom windows and saw several faces peering down at her. Feeling bad, she wished Miss Lindsay could rescue them all. Lily waved up at them as they began to drive away.

Miss Lindsay glanced across at Lily, saying, 'You've told me that Jo is pregnant too and I understand that what she's told you must be a terrible shock but we need to take stock here and remember that you made your decision months ago that you didn't want Tom or the baby.'

'I know, Miss Lindsay. It's just that I feel so betrayed by both of them. They are the two people in the world that I thought cared about me.' Misery swept over her again and she held back a sob.

'Try to see it from their point of view, Lily; they may see it that you deserted them.'

This was a sobering thought and Lily could see that maybe they could feel that way. Even so, she still felt replaced and abandoned. 'It was the self-satisfied look on her face that really upset me. She didn't have to gloat.'

'Lily, listen to me, I understand you're upset but you have a lot to face in the next two weeks. You need to keep strong for the birth. I'm really glad that Mrs Jenkins can take you, she's very kind. You will be much happier there. It's not long now Lily and you can put all this behind you.'

Lily listened to what she was saying and knew that she had to continue to be strong to get through this last bit. Tom and Jo could go to hell; she would have to concentrate on what was happening to herself and her baby. She suddenly realised that she hadn't thought about the baby for a while, only that she wanted it to be over. Now it was her reality that she had to face. 'Is it painful giving birth?'

'I believe for most people it is. You will have doctors and midwives to help you and they will give you something for the pain if it gets too bad.'

She didn't want to think about that now. 'How long before we get there?'

'About twenty minutes. You'll be in time for dinner and the cooking always smells good there.'

They settled into silence for the rest of the journey, Lily now recognising parts of Tunbridge Wells. Looking at the stately old buildings, she started to feel better and found herself enjoying the regal feel of the town. They turned into a driveway that was short and steep and the home had the look of a normal residence. It was red clinker brick with a few steps up to a veranda and the front door. It looked homely but Lily still had a rush of apprehension. There would be a new matron and lots of new girls to get used to. For a second she regretted leaving the familiar behind but a picture of Miss Simms sprang into her mind and she shuddered.

People were coming out to greet them. There was a kindly looking, middle-aged woman and some heavily pregnant girls. They looked friendly and Lily was stunned at the contrast to where she'd just come from.

'Lily, meet Mrs Jenkins and the girls.'

They all said hello and introduced themselves as they walked into the home. Lily felt she was genuinely welcome and didn't know what to make of it. Mrs Jenkins showed them to Lily's dormitory. It was a long room with four beds. It looked cosy and Lily breathed a sigh of relief.

'I'll let Jessie and Miranda show you around, Lily. I have to get back to the kitchen and help Mrs Wright with the dinner. It will be ready in half an hour.'

'Thanks, Mrs Jenkins. It smells fabulous. Thank you for taking me in at such short notice.'

'That's all right. You'll be happy here. We're like a big family. You'll see.' She reached over and squeezed Lily's hand, looked over at Miss Lindsay as if to say, all's well, and disappeared out the door and down the hallway.

'Lily, I have to get going,' said Miss Lindsay. 'You'll be in good hands here. Do you feel you'll be okay?'

'Yes, thank you. It's so nice of you to do this for me. Thanks for putting yourself out. I'm sorry I was so upset this afternoon.' She felt ashamed and tears pricked her eyes again.

'I wanted to help you. You'll be better off here. I'll phone your parents when I get home to let them know we have moved you.'

Lily winced at the thought of Miss Lindsay having to tell her parents. She tried not to think of them at all. She was having a knee-jerk reaction of panic as she was to be left once more in a strange place but checked it in time. She took a breath and realised she would be okay here. It felt safe.

'I will ring you on Monday, Lily, to see if you've settled in, okay?' She gave Lily a hug and then ran down the steps to her car.

Twenty-two

The sound of laughter greeted Lily as she walked into the dining room, trailing one of the girls. Everyone was getting seated around a long pine dining table. There were only about fifteen girls and two staff. They looked relaxed and Lily thought she should pinch herself in case she was dreaming. She had never had dinner in such a convivial way. The closest was at school when she and her friends had lunch.

'All right, Lily?' asked Mrs Jenkins as her friendly blue eyes sought hers.

'Yes, I am, thank you, Mrs Jenkins. Everything is really good. The food looks and smells too good to be true.'

Feeling her shoulders relax, she began to enjoy her chicken curry and rice. It was the best food she'd had in weeks. The only time she'd had curry before was at an Indian restaurant but never when it was cooked in someone's home kitchen. The girls were very inquisitive about a new girl arriving so suddenly and late in the day. They bombarded her with questions, looking for some gossip to add excitement to their lives. She filled them in as honestly as she could, careful to leave out the betrayal by Tom and Jo. They knew there was more to her story but they could wait until she was ready to tell it. Mrs Jenkins gently chided them. 'Come on, girls; let's give the girl a chance to eat her food. You can ask her questions later.'

After dinner everyone mucked in and took away plates and helped wash up. Then they all piled into the common room to watch TV. *Top of the Pops* was on and Lily stared at the screen. It seemed alien to her now, as if it was another lifetime when she loved to watch the program. She realised she wasn't the young girl who watched the bands every week with excitement and anticipation of where life would take her. No, thought Lily, I'm nine months pregnant and have no-one in this world who gives a damn.

She continued watching but it gave her no pleasure anymore. Once again she had the odd feeling that she was watching herself watching TV. She was glad when it was a suitable time to say she was tired and wanted to go to bed. Everyone wished her 'goodnight' and she felt fifteen pairs of eyes on her as she left the room. She took her time getting herself ready for bed and putting her few things away. She had less now than she did three months ago.

Lily lay there trying to get to sleep but her eyes kept flying open and she felt wide awake. For the first time in a long while, she allowed herself to think of Tom. It had been safer not to think of him for the last few months. She wondered again why she'd agreed to stay at Tom's house on Saturday nights. It had obviously been a recipe for disaster. What an idiot she'd been. It had been nearly nine months now so she knew she had to get over it. Her mind drifted to the first time she had lay in bed with Tom. How he held her tightly, telling her how much he loved her. He had kissed her gently and held her with tenderness. She hadn't felt he'd been pressuring her into sex. She had felt closer to him in that moment than she had ever felt to another person before. It had been an irresistible force and she hadn't been able to hold her distance, emotionally or physically. It seemed a lifetime ago. She had thrown everything away that she had been dreaming of and her anger and despair had stopped her from remembering why. She didn't feel like crying anymore. She just wanted to think it all through, as if she now had space to breathe. The thought landed in her head that she needed to write to Tom. Feeling a sense of urgency, she carefully got out of bed, picked up her bag and tiptoed out of the room. It was late and her three roommates were all sleeping. She made her way to the common room and hoped she would find paper there. The place was relatively small and she wasn't too far from it. After feeling around for the light switch and turning it on, she started to look in the cupboards and desk for paper. Lily felt a bit furtive as she went through the desk drawers but then finding a pad, she plonked herself heavily down into an armchair. She rummaged in her bag for her pen and then began:

Dear Tom,

I'm sorry that I have shut you out. I couldn't read your letters as nothing they could have said was going to make what I had to go through any better. I had to do it alone. My father would not have let you near our house anyway. It's been hell.

I was in an unmarried mothers' home near Maidstone and it was run by an evil woman who liked to make our lives a total misery. I couldn't take it anymore and the social worker has brought me to this place in Tunbridge Wells. It's so much nicer here. I wish I had asked her to move me weeks ago. Hardly anyone has come to see me. My brother brought my mum once and he brought my little brother another time. Jo came yesterday. She said that you two are going to get married. Is that true?

Anyway, doesn't really matter. My baby is due within the next week or so. Mrs Jenkins reckons I'm so large and so distressed, that she's going to make an appointment for me with a doctor at Pembury Hospital as soon as they can fit me in. She's suggesting I should ask them to induce me (bring the baby on sooner). I'm so fed up with it, I'm going to ask.

If you want to come and see me, it would be okay. I'll get them to let you know when the baby is born

*if you want. No-one else will come to the hospital so
it might be nice to see someone. Anyway, up to you.
The phone number here is*—Lily pushed herself
up out of the chair and walked slowly over to
the black telephone and peered at the number
on the dial—*823591. Hope you're okay.*

Love Lily

She slumped back in the chair, suddenly feeling very
tired. Looking around, she saw a clock on the wall saying
one thirty. Yawning, she re-read the letter a couple of
times. Deciding it was okay she neatly folded it and put
it in her bag. She would post it tomorrow. Feeling more
at peace, she hauled herself out of the chair and made
her way back to the bedroom, being careful to turn off
the light. She marvelled that she would never have dared
roam around in the middle of the night at Craigmore.

Twenty-three

L ily awoke to the birds singing and the sun coming through the curtains. She looked around her, feeling groggy for a moment. She wondered where she was. It felt so peaceful; she thought she might have died and gone to heaven. Once her eyes focused, she remembered. She stretched and luxuriated in being allowed to stay in bed until she woke up. Propping herself up on one elbow, she looked to see if the others were still sleeping. Seeing they were, she lay down again, thinking through what had happened and about the impending visit to the doctor. Strangely, she didn't feel so traumatised. It was as if the letter to Tom had been a bridge to a part of her life that she had severed. She wondered if he would reply. She didn't feel too concerned. Her mind was looking forward rather than back for a change. She hoped the doctor agreed to induce her. She'd had enough and wanted to close this long and depressing chapter.

Feeling energised, Lily slid out of bed. She picked up her toiletry bag and made her way quietly out of the room. Three sleepy faces looked up at her. They all greeted her with; 'Hi, Lily!'; 'Hi, Lily! Are you okay?'; 'Hi, Lily!'

Lily smiled at them. 'Yeah, I'm much better, thanks.'

Mrs Jenkins let Lily know at breakfast that she had made an appointment for her for Thursday morning. 'We'll leave at nine thirty, Lily.'

'That's a big relief, thank you. I will have time to relax a bit. I have a letter that I want to post and I wonder if there is a post office nearby.'

'Not a post office but there is a post box just down the road. I can give you a stamp if you need one.'

'A stamp will be brilliant. I'm sorry to be a nuisance but could I have an envelope too?'

Jessie piped up, 'I have an envelope you can have, Lily, and I'll show you where the post box is, if you like.'

'There, everything is working out for you. You can just put your feet up for a few days.'

❋

On Thursday morning Lily and Mrs Jenkins drove to the hospital. Lily was eager and nervous at the same time. Mrs Jenkins went in with Lily to see the young doctor.

'Yes, you're definitely full term so we'll take you in now and induce you. Then you will be okay to go back with Mrs Jenkins and wait until the labour starts. How does that sound?'

She nearly shouted yes! She was so eager to get it happening. She didn't even know what she was agreeing to. She only knew this would make the baby come quicker.

Only the baby didn't seem to want to come quicker. It took a day for her water to break and another few hours before she started getting pains and was able to get ready to go back to the hospital. She thought the baby just didn't want to come out and she didn't blame it. She wondered if her baby had been feeling all the anguish and anger that she had been continually going through. A thought swiftly followed that maybe she knew her mother was going to give her away to strangers. Tears welled up. Lily tried to send her baby thoughts that she would be better off. It seemed hopeless. She felt unconvinced that this one message could help reassure an unborn baby that things would turn out all right after her mother had been experiencing fear and trauma for nine months. Brushing a tear away, Lily picked up her case, braced her shoulders and went out to the driveway.

They eased her carefully into the car and took her back to the hospital at the top of Pembury Road. It was about a mile further up the hill than Lily's old school. Gritting her teeth through a contraction, she turned her head as they went past the school, feeling angry that she was on her way to a hospital to have a baby and not at school. She wondered if Jo was in there. The pain took over and mercifully obliterated all thought. They were worse than anything she could have imagined. She did the breathing she had been taught and hoped like hell it would pass quickly.

As she was admitted into the maternity wing she said, ''Bye, and thanks, Mrs Jenkins, you've been really kind to me.'

'That's all right, Lily, it's been good to have you with us. Take care now. I hope everything turns out well for you.'

She walked away and Lily felt alone again. As if hearing her thought, Mrs Jenkins abruptly turned and called out to her, 'Lily, I forgot to tell you, a young man called late last night. Said he had received a letter from you. Name's Tom. He said he would ring again in his lunch break. What shall I tell him?'

Lily stopped and walked back, oblivious to the irritation of the young nurse who was leading her away. 'Can you tell him where I am and say he can ring here to see if the baby has arrived?'

'Well, that won't be long by the look of it. I'll tell him to ring tonight, okay?'

'Thanks again, Mrs Jenkins, I do appreciate all you've done for me.' She turned back to the nurse and was put in a wheelchair and wheeled away. She realised that Tom must have rung as soon as he got the letter. She wondered what he wanted to say.

She didn't want to start thinking about Tom and was hoping another contraction would come. It was then she realised she hadn't had one since she got here. Not knowing anything about labour pains or births, Lily could only assume they would start up again soon. The nurses lay her on a half table, half bed, Lily didn't know what it was, but it was high, maybe like an operating table. They told her they would come back with the midwife. It was a large room that looked like an operating room. There were all sorts of contraptions around her. It wasn't what she imagined a birthing room to be.

After what seemed about half an hour the nurse returned with a plump, middle-aged midwife saying, 'Now, young lady, my name is Mrs Mills. Let's see what's happening here. You were induced two days ago and your water broke about eight this morning. Is that correct?' She had a brisk, no-nonsense manner.

'Yes, that's right.'

'You're another lass from the home?'

'Yes. Mrs Jenkins brought me in.'

'Ah. A fine woman. Now, how often are the contractions?'

'They were about every three minutes but I haven't had one for the last half an hour or so.'

'I see. I'll examine you now and we'll see what's going on.' Frowning, she began pushing on Lily's belly. It was very uncomfortable whatever the midwife was doing and she grimaced and wriggled involuntarily. 'Stay still as you can, please, dear.'

Lily grimaced again but forced herself not to move.

'Right, everything seems normal. We'll leave you here for a while and see if the contractions start up again. If not, dearie, you'll be going back to the home for the night.'

Her words shocked Lily. Panicky thoughts followed; they couldn't just send her back, could they? Surely the baby is meant to come out now. She didn't want to show her ignorance by asking. She realised, miserably, that she really should have read up on this business of birthing instead of ignoring it. Some of the girls seemed to be reading baby books all the time but she hadn't felt she'd wanted to. 'Bollocks!' She swore into the empty room. She'd always thought that knowledge was power and had said it often to others. Now she felt stupid because of her lack of knowledge about giving birth. The midwife and both nurses had walked out and she was left alone, lying there in the silence. She strained her ears and could hear faint, squeaking footsteps going up and down on the linoleum floor outside and occasionally, muffled voices.

She must have dozed off because a contraction suddenly gripped her and forgetting where she was, she moved suddenly and nearly fell off the table. She panted and willed it to pass. She could see a clock on the wall and thought it would be wise to time them so she could tell the midwife when she came back. They kept coming and coming, getting more intense, but no-one had come in to check on her. She began to worry that they had forgotten about her. She didn't want to be alone and she was feeling really scared. Another twenty minutes went by and a nurse came in and asked, 'How are you getting on? Do you have contractions now?'

'I'm getting them every three minutes again.'

'Good. Well done. I'll check on you in another twenty minutes and we'll see how close they are then.' She went out and the door closed with a soft squish behind her.

Lily became more anxious due to their lack of concern. She wondered how bad they have to be until they take it seriously.

It seemed like hours went by. The pain got worse but the contractions evidently weren't coming fast enough. The nurses offered her food but she didn't want any. She took a sip of water as her mouth was dry. They popped in and out but Lily lost track of how often. It was eleven o'clock at night; she had been in labour for fifteen hours. The midwife had checked her cervix a couple of times and had said the baby wasn't close enough yet.

'Tell me, why am I sweating and in terrible pain then?' Lily asked angrily.

'It happens sometimes, dear, that the baby just isn't quite ready to come out. Don't worry; he or she will come when they're ready, can't be much more than three or four hours now.'

She dozed and then the pain would come again. After another hour, Lily was screaming and swearing at the top of her voice. She felt she was being ripped from the inside. Her eyes focused on the fake wedding ring that she had been advised to buy and with a burst of anger she tore it off her finger and threw it across the room in frustration, shouting, 'Stupid poxy ring! I don't want it! Too bad what anyone thinks!' She'd bought it in Woolworths months ago and had put it on that morning. It looked ridiculous and gaudy. A nurse came in. They were all different and Lily was beyond recognising them.

'What's all this noise about? You're going to have to be more quiet, Lily, it's midnight.'

'I don't care,' Lily shouted. 'Get me the midwife or a doctor now. I want to know why this baby isn't coming out.'

The nurse took one look at Lily's angry, red and sweating face and rushed out saying, 'I'll get one now.'

A different midwife came. Through Lily's haze she registered that the other one had probably buggered off home hours ago and was cosily tucked up in bed by now. She was examined again.

'The baby is definitely not ready yet. We'll have to wait.'

'I can't wait!' Lily screamed again at the top of her lungs. 'You all keep buggering off and leaving me alone. I could bloody well die here and no-one would know!'

'Keep your voice down, young lady, there are other women here in labour too, you know.'

'No, I won't keep my voice down. Get me something for the pain then.' She kept on shouting at the top of her voice. She didn't care. She only cared about the unbearable pain and getting the baby out.

'We can give you an epidural for the pain. Do you want that?'

Lily had no clue what an epidural was but shouted, 'If it helps the pain, I'll have it.'

'I'll get nurse to prepare one now. She'll be back in a few minutes. Try to calm down.'

'Easy for you to say,' Lily spat.

When the nurse got back, Lily could see it was a very big needle. She hated needles.

'Where are you going to put that?'

There were two of them looking at her as if she was a mad woman.

'We will turn you on your side and put it into the base of your spine. You won't be able to feel much but as the baby could still take a few more hours it will have time to wear off before you need to push.'

It sounded very drastic. 'I don't think it will be a few more hours before the baby comes.'

The nurse looked at her with a sympathetic half smile on her face as if to say you poor, ignorant girl, we know best. Well, Lily hoped they did know best. She didn't have much confidence so far.

She felt the effects of the needle straight away. It relaxed her. The nurses said that they would be back to check on her in twenty minutes or so. Lily looked at the clock. It was half-past midnight and she would be checking that they kept their word.

'Well, they're not bloody well keeping their word.' She felt an even stronger contraction tear through her. The pain was dulled but it still made her want to scream. She thought that she must have done so because the nurse came running in. It was one a.m.

'You're ten minutes late,' she shouted accusingly. 'Get the bloody doctor, the baby's coming!'

'I can assure you it's not, Lily. Mrs Webb is an excellent midwife and if she says you have three hours to go then you can be sure that's what it will be.'

'Well, I'm not bloody sure, so go and get her now!'

She screamed it out as loud as she could and would go on screaming until someone took her seriously. The nurse rushed out again and came back two minutes later with Mrs Webb.

'Now what's all this fuss? You're not the only one here having a baby tonight, you know. You must control yourself.'

Lily felt more enraged that this calm, superior woman was telling her what to do when she had been in this terrible pain for more than sixteen hours now. 'I don't care what you say. The baby's coming. I can feel it.'

The midwife tsked, saying, 'I doubt you can feel anything much, you only had the epidural an hour ago.' She started to check Lily's cervix. 'Oh, my goodness! The baby is coming. How can this be happening? Nurse, go and get Dr Lee immediately and tell him about the epidural and that the baby is coming. Tell him to authorise the antidote or this mother will not be able to push.'

'Yes, Mrs Webb.'

Suddenly there was action in her room. At last, she thought.

Within minutes she heard footsteps running and a doctor burst in. He looked at Mrs Webb, checked Lily's cervix and immediately injected her with the antidote. 'Let's hope this works swiftly enough, Mrs Webb, for Miss Davis to be able to push the baby out.'

He sounded condemning of the midwife. Serves her bloody well right, Lily thought venomously as another contraction, making her want to push, went through her. She heard the doctor's voice.

'Now you may feel like you need to push but I'm afraid you must hold back. Unfortunately, the baby's head will not be able to get through your opening and I am going to have to cut you so that you don't tear. Don't be alarmed, you won't feel anything. Do you understand, Miss Davis? Nurse Braithwaite, anaesthetic and scissors please.'

Before Lily had time to consider the ramifications of what Dr Lee had said, she felt a cold swab of something over her vagina and within minutes, the awful sound of cutting. It sounded to Lily exactly the same as when you were slicing slowly and methodically through heavy material with dressmaking scissors. Lily closed her eyes and wondered if this horrific nightmare could get any worse.

'Now, don't push until we tell you. Is that clear?' Dr Lee was frowning and seemed concerned which only made Lily's fears get to fever pitch.

'If I hadn't been bloody well left on my own for hours at a time we wouldn't be in this mess,' Lily hissed.

Dr Lee and Mrs Webb exchanged glances. Mrs Webb piped up that they were very short staffed. Lily's legs were up and apart. The doctor and midwife took turns to anxiously look in between them.

'I can see the head! Look, Dr Lee!'

Dr Lee ducked his head and then looked up at Lily. 'Miss Davis, I want you to push, can you do that?'

Although her eyesight had become hazy through dripping sweat and exhaustion, she could see he looked worried. Lily pushed with all her might. It's what she'd wanted to do for hours.

'It's working! Good girl!'

The praise sounded absurd to Lily, as if she had passed a test and was going to get a pat on the head. The urge to push again obliterated thought. She screamed and grunted and pushed with all her strength.

'Thank God the antidote worked so fast.'

Lily's ears must have been tired as the talking seemed far away. Suddenly, Mrs Webb said eagerly to Dr Lee, 'It's here! The baby's here!' She sounded excited as if this wasn't an everyday occurrence for her.

'Don't push anymore, Lily. We'll take over now.' Dr Lee's voice was kind.

She slumped back on her pillows, glad to be told she didn't need to do anymore.

'You can take over now, Mrs Webb. That's a very healthy baby girl we have here.' He seemed pleased his job was done and left the room.

'Lily, sit up and look at your baby. It's a girl and she's beautiful.'

Lily didn't want to. All babies looked the same, with red, screwed-up faces. She didn't need to look.

'Lily!' Mrs Webb sounded insistent. She came around and put her arm under Lily's back and pushed her up so she could see the baby lying across her ankles. She took in a sharp breath. Her baby didn't have a red face and it looked straight into her eyes with its own round blue ones. It felt as though her baby was looking into her soul. Lily heard the thought, don't give me away!

She shook her head a little. She must be delirious. She looked again and her baby's eyes, looking into her own, were steady and a clear blue. The colour of a summer sky, Lily thought. Shaken, she tore her eyes away from her baby's stare.

'There, dear, you have a lovely baby daughter. Would you like to hold her before we take her away?'

Lily was torn. The baby would be taken from her in three days, best not to get close, but she said, 'Yes!' Carefully taking the tiny bundle in her arms and looking down at her daughter, Lily felt awed that this delicate, beautiful baby was created inside of her. Then they took her baby away, telling her that someone would be coming to stitch her up soon. Lying on the pillows, she closed her eyes, thinking she could rest at last, but they reluctantly opened again when the nurse came back and wiped her face with a wet cloth and generally cleaned her up.

'You need to be stitched up. An intern will come and do it in about twenty minutes, okay? I'll get you ready by putting your feet in stirrups. Okay, Lily?'

Lily was sleepy, but she said, 'Okay,' to the nurse. She lay resting for a while but then her mind started to engage, thinking, what if I did keep my baby? Either I'm going mad or she implored me not to give her away. She didn't know what to do. If this was another message from her soul, she didn't think she should ignore it. Looking at the clock, she could see that it was two thirty a.m. She wanted to sleep but had to wait until they stitched her up before she would be in a comfortable bed. She dozed for a while and then startled awake when she heard the door open. She glanced automatically up at the clock. It was twenty past three. She was shocked that they had left her bleeding for over an hour. The intern introduced himself as Ned. He smiled and said, 'How're you doing?'

He was very young and handsome. It seemed that all young doctors were handsome. She wondered if it was a sign, like don't throw your life away; there are lots of handsome, intelligent young men out there and one will be for you one day. But the look her baby had given her was haunting her. As the intern began stitching Lily up, he told her that she needed about twenty stitches. She digested that awful bit of information but then before she could stop herself she started telling him her story and that now she didn't know what to do and what did he think she should do? After listening for nearly half an hour, he said, 'I don't know what is best for you to do but there's a social worker who comes on duty at six a.m. and she would be able to help you.'

'That's probably the wisest thing to do. Thank you.' She looked at the clock: four a.m. Only two hours to go and I can sort this out. She felt comforted that she was going to be able to talk to someone who would be in a position to help.

Ned told her that he was nearly finished and she would be able to sleep soon. She was glad that whatever he had injected her with worked so well that she felt no pain at all. It just seemed that she was having a conversation with the top of a young man's head. He was busy doing what he had to do and after a while it didn't seem so odd that his head was bent down in between her legs.

He had a lovely voice and it had made her feel better to have an interaction with a sensitive and intelligent person after being in a virtual prison.

Minutes after he left, two nurses came in and wheeled her to a ward that was down a long corridor. They put her in a clean nightgown and then wanted to put her under the covers. She told them that she was worried that she would go into a deep sleep if she was too comfortable and miss the social worker at six so they left her on top of the bed. Her eyes kept closing but she'd force them open and kept looking at the clock on the wall.

Twenty-four

Lily wasn't normally physically brave. She would have loved to have snuggled under the covers, to close her eyes and be able to sleep. There was no choice; this was the most important decision she was ever likely to make. She knew that the stitches and everything else was going to hurt like hell when she got herself off the bed and walked down the corridor but she would have to put up with it.

The minute hand hovered just before the twelve, making it nearly six a.m. She eased herself off the bed. The nurses had described where the office was and she hobbled down the corridor. She saw the name Smyth and 'Social Worker' under it and tapped on the door. It opened immediately and Lily saw a tall woman in her later years with soft, wrinkled skin, kindly grey-blue eyes and wearing a white coat. Lily searched her face and decided she looked like someone whose advice she could trust. 'I'm Lily Davis, I've just had a baby and I need your help.'

'Nice to meet you, Lily, I'm Mrs Smyth, come in and sit down. Nurse told me you were coming. How can I help you?'

Lily told her the whole sad and sorry story. Tears poured down her cheeks but she hardly noticed them. When she got to the bit about the baby imploring her not to give her away, she hesitated and felt stupid but it had to be told. Mrs Smyth nodded a lot and looked sympathetic. When Lily had finished she asked, 'Lily, do you love Tom?'

Straight away she answered, 'I don't think I do but it's been difficult to know what I feel when I've been so worried about my best friend's feelings.'

'Does he still love you?'

'I believe he does. He loved me so much I can't believe he could just turn it off like that.'

'Well, if he loves you that much and you do marry him, I think that he would have enough love for both of you and in time you would grow to love him.'

Lily frowned and a feeling of panic came over her. 'But what if I meet someone later that I fall in love with?'

'If you don't look you won't find.'

The words sounded wise and Lily contemplated them for a moment. It seemed like good advice so she said, 'Thank you for all that you've told me. I don't know what Tom will think about it but he will probably come in to see us soon and I'll see what he wants.'

Mrs Smyth put her hand on Lily's shoulder. 'You're a brave young girl to consider taking this on. I'm here if you need me again.'

Lily felt undeserving of the praise. She gave Mrs Smyth a weak smile and hobbled gingerly back up the corridor again, feeling delirious with tiredness. Mrs Smyth's words were going around in her head. As she got within sight of her bed she saw a small pink crib beside it. They'd brought her back. She felt excited and her feelings of a moment ago dropped away from her like a heavy cloak. She walked up quietly and peeked in. Sleeping peacefully on her side was a baby so pretty she looked like a doll. She had lots of dark hair and long black eyelashes that swept down onto her cheek. Lily felt a pang as her exhaustion took over and she got into bed. She didn't dare touch her fragile-looking baby in case she woke her. She had to sleep.

'Wake up, Lily!'

She could hear the baby's distressed crying as she dragged herself up from a deep level of sleep.

'Baby Davis has to be fed.'

She pushed herself up and the nurse adjusted her pillows. 'Now, dear, we understand your baby is for adoption so you have the choice of breastfeeding her for three days or, our advice would be to bottle feed her. It's better for them anyway and that way you won't get so attached.'

'Oh! All right, I'll bottle feed her then.' She realised she didn't have a clue about this either. She felt a wave of sadness and wished her mother was there to help her.

They had a bottle ready and gave her the crying baby. Her tiny face was scrunched up and her little mouth was all pink gums, wide open making that wah, wah sound that Lily had been convinced babies made all the time. She took the bottle and listened to the nurse telling her what to do. She was apprehensive but it was logical that you had to keep the bottle tipped upward so the baby didn't gulp down air. She soon got the hang of it. The feelings that rippled through her were indescribable as she looked down at her daughter in her arms, in wonder. Her baby was now quiet and angelic-looking again. Lily looked up surreptitiously to see what other mothers were doing. Those that were feeding or holding their babies seemed besotted with dreamy, happy looks on their faces. She wondered what they thought of her, an unmarried mother in their midst? She looked back at her baby and knew she didn't care.

Lily realised she couldn't keep thinking of her as 'the baby', she would have to give her the name she had chosen. She had decided on a name during all those dark, cold months of winter when she had huddled under the covers in her bed, either staring at the ceiling or closing her eyes in fear and despair. She had prayed for a girl and she had chosen one name only: Cilla, after the singer, Cilla Black. Cilla's song 'Anyone Who Had a Heart' was a favourite. She sang it quietly to herself: 'Anyone who had a heart could look at me and know that I love you'. She felt a tear slide down her cheek as she realised how true that was now. She pulled up her shoulder so that she could wipe the tear away and said, 'Hello, Cilla.'

Cilla opened her eyes a little and then closed them as if she was content now that she was being held close in her mother's arms. A feeling of pure love filled Lily's heart. It was love like she had never experienced before. It wasn't trying to get love from a parent or a friend or a boyfriend and then hoping that it would be safe to love them too. It was just love coming out of her with no fear that she would not be loved in return. She felt fiercely protective towards her innocent baby. Lily knew she did not want Cilla to ever have to go through the pain and rejection that she had gone through in her short life.

'I don't know how we're going to do this, Cilla, but I think everything's going to be all right.'

As she looked down at her daughter she thought that Cilla suited her perfectly. A nurse's quick and squeaky footsteps made her look up. She was short and plump with carrot red hair escaping from under her white cap. She had a kind but determined expression on her pale, freckled face, saying, 'Let's show you how to burp the wind out of the baby and then we'll lay her down for another sleep. It's ten a.m., Lily, get some more sleep yourself. We'll take the baby if she cries again. Lunch is at twelve.'

Lily was reluctant to hand Cilla over after she had successfully got her to burp up some wind but knew she had to get more sleep. Gratefully she allowed the nurse to take the small, warm bundle and snuggled down again.

It seemed no sooner had she got to sleep than something made her stir and wake up again. She looked up over the covers and saw Tom coming towards her.

He was grinning from ear to ear as he looked across at her. She knew in that instant that he still loved her and everything would be all right after all. She expected him to keep walking to her but he stopped in his tracks at the crib. The look of adoration on his face as he looked down at his daughter made tears spring to her eyes again. He was beaming with happiness. She knew then that he would be a wonderful father and love their baby.

'Lily! How are you feeling? The baby is beautiful. She looks just like you.'

Lily self-consciously flattened her hair back with her hands as she realised she hadn't looked in a mirror for over twenty-four hours. 'She is amazing, isn't she? She has blue eyes exactly the colour of yours.'

Tom looked chuffed and seemed to stand taller. He pulled the visitor's chair closer to the side of the bed and sat down. There was an awkward moment as they faced each other after all this time and all that had gone on. They both started to speak at the same time and then both stopped again. It made them laugh. In the silence that followed, Lily took the opportunity to ask him the question that had been making her so angry. 'Why did Jo tell me that you are going to get married?'

Tom shifted in his chair and looked uncomfortable with her steady gaze on him. 'It's hard to explain. I loved you so much and I thought we could get married and be happy bringing our baby into the world. I could understand your anger, Lily, but I was devastated when you rejected me. I couldn't eat or sleep. I didn't want to go out. I had to change jobs 'cause the blokes at work kept taking the piss out of me. You didn't answer any of my letters and by the time Jo started to come and visit me at work, I had given up hope. I started to meet her at the pub and ...' He averted his eyes and looked down at the floor; he looked close to tears. 'Well, you know, one thing led to another and when Jo got pregnant I felt I couldn't just stand by and let two babies be given away.' He met her gaze but looked away again.

'Did you say you would marry her?'

'I said I would help her and what did she want.'

'Oh. Did you know that she was seeing someone for a few months? Did you ever wonder if it was his?'

'Yeah, I know she had some bloke that was keen on her and took her out a lot but that sort of suited me. I didn't want to get too involved because I still loved you, Lily. Anyway, I felt the baby was probably mine.'

Lily took a sharp intake of breath. Twice she'd heard Tom say that he had loved her in the past tense. 'I am sorry, Tom, but I felt so scared that I just had to run. I wanted to run and not stop until I was as far away as I could get. I truly think it was the only way I could cope.'

'What about now, Lily? Now the baby's here?' He took her hand and it was his turn to search her face for some clue. Lily returned his gaze; after all that she'd been through she didn't feel so scared anymore.

'Now she's here, Tom, I don't want to let her go. Life will never be the same again. I thought I could just take up where I left off but that was a fool's dream. I've named her Cilla.' She thought she saw something like hope leap into Tom's eyes and then he smiled. 'Lily Davis, will you marry me?'

'Yes, Tom, I will.'

He jumped out of the chair and put his arms around her and gave her a long kiss. He sat back down again and held her hand and they just looked at each other as if wondering if this was really happening. Cilla stirred and Tom looked timidly at Lily and said, 'Do you think I could pick her up?'

'I think you should.'

He took the two steps to the crib and looked down, hesitating. Then ever so gently he reached down and took Cilla out of the crib. She was still tightly wrapped in pink cotton and she opened her eyes and looked at Tom. He held her to him and carefully sat down with a look of wonder on his face. 'She's so tiny. What did she weigh?'

'Seven pounds and two ounces.'

He took one of his daughter's hands and held it, stroking the tiny fingers one by one. Lily saw Cilla's fingers curl around his little finger. Tom looked at Lily and they stayed silent, not wanting to break the spell.

Tom came back again in the evening. He appeared more confident as he walked towards her bed. As before, he stopped and looked down at the sleeping Cilla and seemed reluctant to drag his eyes from her. But as he took the last two steps to Lily he fished something out of his pocket. Lily drew in a breath when she saw it was a small diamond engagement ring. He beamed as he put the ring on her finger. Lily felt this was all unreal. Like she was in a play, playing a part. She didn't quite know what was going to happen next but she was willing to be prompted as it went along. They didn't say much. Neither of them knew what to say anyway. Tom couldn't resist picking up Cilla and they sat quietly, admiring their baby that had brought them together again.

'When do you get out of here?'

'They said I have to stay in here ten days to get my strength back and to learn how to look after a baby.'

'You do look very pale and tired. Did it take long for Cilla to be born?'

'It took so long I thought she was never going to come out. I think it was seventeen or eighteen hours.'

'Bloody hell, Lily! No wonder you look so tired. Was it very painful?'

'It was more painful than I could ever describe. I was frightened and most of the time didn't have anyone in the room with me. I got really angry because they kept telling me she wasn't coming and I could feel that she was. I think I've got twenty-four stitches.'

She saw Tom wince.

'Anyway, it was worth it.'

'It certainly was.' He proudly looked down at Cilla in his arms.

'All right, I'll go now and let you get some sleep and I'll come back tomorrow night. We'll work out what to do then. Okay?' He carefully got up and gently put Cilla back in her crib, then gave Lily a gentle kiss on the lips as if he thought she was fragile after finding out what she had been through. ''Bye, Lily.'

She was relieved that he wasn't staying for too long; it had been a very big day.

❀

Tom was her only visitor for the first three days. Lily didn't mind, she needed time to rest and get herself back together. The routine was soothing and she felt well looked after. One evening, at the start of visitors' hour, Lily was surprised to see Simon and her mother walking into the ward.

'Hello, Lily! Surprised to see us? How are you getting on?'

Before she could answer Simon, she saw her mother look at her and then stop at the crib and gaze down at her granddaughter. She started to say something but it caught in her throat as if she were about to cry. 'Hello, Lily, can I pick her up?'

'Hello, Mum, of course you can.'

Jill Davis put her handbag down on the floor and then carefully picked up the sleeping baby and held her tenderly in her arms. Lily could tell there would be no argument from her mother at least. She also noted that her father was conspicuously absent but that was no surprise at all and was even a relief. Lily relaxed and was pleased they had come.

'Was it difficult to come and see me, Mum?'

'You know what your dad's like, Lily. There was a shouting match and he said that I wasn't to go but Simon was coming and I couldn't stay home. I told him you're my daughter, his too. He could either come with us or stay there. He just huffed and puffed like he does so I put my coat on and walked out the door.'

Lily saw her mother's worried face soften as she held Cilla.

'Mum, Tom came to see me twice the day Cilla was born; he still loves me and asked me to marry him.' She looked from her mother to Simon, gauging their reaction. 'I said yes!'

Their eyes widened at this turn of events.

'I love my baby and Tom does too. He gave me this engagement ring.' Lily shyly pulled her hand out from under the covers so her mother could see the ring.

Jill Davis's expression went from disbelief to possibly pleased. She carefully put Cilla down in the crib and said, 'You realise that boy is going to have to come and ask your father if he can marry you, don't you?'

Lily gulped. The thought of Tom, who was almost half the size of her father, fronting up to him and saying that he would like to marry his daughter seemed a ridiculous scenario.

'Let's think about that later, Mum. Will I be allowed to bring Cilla home in a week?'

'Oh, Lily, let me work on him. He's been wallpapering and painting your room. I'm not sure what he'll think of you keeping the baby.' She looked worried again.

'It'll work out, Mum. I don't know how but it will.'

Simon ventured, 'We'll work on him, Lily. We'd better get going now.' He walked to the crib and looked down at her baby. The lines across his forehead softened. 'She's beautiful, Lily. 'Bye now, I'll come in again soon,' he said gently.

She looked up at him and nodded. He was tall with jet black hair like their father but his face was finer featured and kind, more like their mother's. She felt distant though, as if these were just more characters in the play. She felt tired and closed her eyes. ''Bye then. Thanks for bringing Mum.'

❁

Tom came every day and even brought her flowers. They were pink lilies. They smelled wonderful and she marvelled that they must have been grown in a hot house.

Gradually, with a lot of practice and coaching from the nurses, she learned how to take care of Cilla. It was a huge relief that she was fortunate enough to have the mothering instinct. Some poor mothers evidently didn't get it. It would be an impossible task without it.

Five days before she was due to be released from hospital, her neighbours, Sylvie and Fred, came in to see her. They fussed around her and Sylvie clucked and cooed at the baby in delight. 'Oh, you dear little thing.'

As she held Cilla in her arms, Sylvie, a big woman with a large bosom and a chin hanging down where her throat should be, enveloped Cilla so that she almost disappeared from view. Lily loved that she had a big heart and that kindness always shone out from her. Mr Higgs was hovering behind his wife like a nervous bird. He was the exact contrast to his wife, only around five feet six inches tall and very thin. He had a wide smile and twinkly blue eyes. Although incongruous to look at, they made a happy couple.

'When are you coming home with this dear little baby, Lily?'

'I can't come home; evidently Dad won't have us there.'

Sylvie narrowed her eyes and said, 'God! He's a mean old bugger! Well, you come and live with us then until the old sod changes his mind.'

Lily looked up at Mr Higgs and he was nodding his head and smiling in agreement. Feeling teary, she said, 'Thank you, Sylvie, thanks, Fred. You've always been so kind to me. I don't think I would have survived all these years without the both of you being there for me.'

'That's settled then. We'll ask the nurse when you can leave and we'll be here to get you.' With that she got up, carefully lay Cilla down in her crib and said,

'Come on, Fred, let's go home and get a room ready for these poor little mites.' They kissed her on the cheek and then Sylvie was off down the ward with Fred hurrying along behind her.

Lily was left feeling that this play was getting stranger every day. Then a wave of excitement went through her. I'm leaving here! I have somewhere to go. Tom had told her not to worry and that he was finding a house for them to live in and that his cousin Marg was helping him arrange the wedding. It would be in three weeks' time at the Tunbridge Wells Registry Office. She lay back on her pillows and smiled. For once in her life she didn't have to do anything. She could just allow herself to be carried along with it.

❁

Sylvie and Fred came in five days later as promised. Lily was dressed in the skirt and large blouse that she had worn many months ago, when she had been picked up by Miss Lindsay to go into Craigmore. Her case was packed and her baby bundled up for the journey.

It seemed strange arriving in the cul-de-sac and going up the path and turning right instead of left, to someone else's front door. She felt relieved that she didn't yet have to face her father. She waited for Fred to unlock the front door and they went in. It seemed like home to

Lily anyway. Sarah was there to greet them, and looking as though she didn't know what to make of this strange situation. She peeked at the sleeping baby and smiled. 'Welcome home, Lily!'

It was said as a half joke but tears sprang to Lily's eyes as she was made to face the absurdity of the situation she was in. Sarah still looked young and innocent even though she was three years older than Lily.

Sylvie bustled them through to the kitchen saying, 'I'll put the kettle on, shall I?' Not expecting a reply, she made everyone tea and crumpets. 'Fred! Show Lily up to the spare room so she can get settled.'

Fred jumped up as if he had a spring on his backside and took her case up the stairs, Lily following behind with her precious bundle in her arms. They had made the room look nice with lots of pillows on the bed, a little crib for Cilla and a small vase of flowers picked from their garden on the dressing table. Lily smiled through her tears of gratitude.

After a couple of days, despite their kindness, Lily was starting to feel restless. Mrs Higgs fussed over Cilla constantly and seemed to genuinely enjoy them being there. The weather was warm as it was nearly July. They were having a cup of tea in the kitchen one day and Sylvie had Cilla in her arms as usual. She said cheerily, 'I'm going to take the little one out for some fresh air. Come on, Cilla; let's see what you think of it out there.'

She walked out through the scullery and out through the back door, in the direction of the back garden. Lily didn't think anything of it until about fifteen minutes later when Sylvie came back; looking flushed in the cheeks, and blurted out triumphantly, 'I took her to see her grandad! You should have seen his face. I said, "Shame on you, Bill! You have a beautiful little grand-daughter here and you haven't even seen her. Look at her! Go on look!" He was puffing on his rollup and wouldn't take his eyes off the wall he was painting but I just put her right under his nose. He put his fag down and looked at her dear little face and I swear he got tears in his eyes. Then I said, "You have to let Lily and this little mite come home." He mumbled like he does and said that looks like what he'll have to do. You can go home, Lily.'

Lily stood looking at Sylvie with a mixture of awe and disbelief on her face. 'You must be the only person I know, Sylvie, that's not frightened of my father.'

'You know me, Lily; I won't take any gyp from anybody, let alone that big bully.'

Fred, looking on proudly at his wife, said, 'There, Lily, you've even got a newly decorated room to go to.'

She thought it was all a miracle really, including the fact that after sixteen years her father had actually taken the time to make her room look pretty.

'Your mum will be over soon for a cup of tea; we'll sort it out then,' Sylvie finished off, still with a big smile on her face.

With a start, Lily realised that this was the day that Tom was coming all the way to Highden to see her father. 'Oh, Sylvie! Tom's coming here today to ask Dad if he can marry me.' Pausing to reflect she added, 'Well, probably better now that Dad has agreed that Cilla and I can go home.'

They all laughed nervously.

Tom knocked on the door a couple of hours later. Lily's mum had already come in and was sitting in an armchair drinking her tea. When Tom saw her he said, 'Ello, Mrs Davis, nice to see you. Ello, Mr and Mrs Higgs! Thanks for taking Lily in.'

Everyone said hello to Tom, looking at him with interest now they knew the purpose of his visit.

'Tom, Sylvie has taken Cilla in and put her under Dad's nose. He's agreed to let us go home.'

Tom eyebrows shot up! Before he could speak, Lily's mother said, 'Tom, if you're going to ask Bill if you can marry Lily, you had better get in there now, whilst there's no-one else there. He's up in Lily's bedroom doing some finishing touches.'

All eyes were on Tom. He looked at them for a moment and then said, 'Okay, wish me luck.' He took a breath, squared his shoulders and walked out of the room, into the hallway, opened the front door, walked down the steps, across the path and knocked loudly on Lily's front door. Jill Davis went to the open front door and called across the path, 'It's open, Tom, just push it and go in.'

She turned back and pulled the Higgs' front door to but didn't shut it. She wanted to cut herself off from whatever was going to happen next but couldn't totally abandon the young boy. They nervously waited, straining their ears for any shouting. No-one could save Tom. Mr Higgs was too small, Lily and her mother wouldn't dare, and Sylvie wouldn't get involved if there was a fight. They could hear the loud ticking of the clock on the mantelpiece in the hushed silence. They waited. After about ten minutes they heard the Davis's door slam and someone come back in through the Higgs' door. Lily ducked her head around the lounge room door. It was Tom and he was smiling. As he walked in everyone was talking at once, asking him what had happened.

'I went upstairs and called out, "Mr Davis?" No answer, so I went up the stairs to Lily's room. He was standing there puffing on a fag. I said, "Hello, Mr Davis! I've come to ask your permission to marry Lily." He kept puffing and then started painting again, and said, without looking at me, "That would probably be best in the circumstances." That was it. I said, "Thanks, I'll look after her." And he mumbled, "Make sure you do," and kept on painting. I stood there for another minute or two but it was like, that's all he's going to say, so I left. I was going to ask him for a beer to celebrate but I thought I'd better not.'

They knew he was joking but the thought of it made them all laugh, taking the tension out of the room. Tom gave Lily a hug and Mr Higgs went off and got some lagers out of the fridge.

That evening, after Tom had caught the train home, Lily packed her few things together and with Sylvie and her mother's help, took herself and Cilla down the steps and across the path to home. Sylvie put the case just inside the door and whispered, 'I'll leave you to it, ducks.

You'll be okay. You know where we are.' And went back out the door, closing it behind her.

Lily stood in the hallway for a moment. She hadn't been in the house for over three months. It felt strange. She could smell the fresh paint. With Cilla in her arms, she pushed open the lounge room door. There, as expected, was her father in his armchair watching TV. She walked up to him and said, 'Dad, I'm home!'

He looked up and said, 'Hello, Lily. Better sit down then.' And went back to watching the TV. Lily thought it was a good result so she sat down and watched TV for a while with her mother and father before saying that she needed to get Cilla's bottle ready.

After boiling the kettle and standing the bottle in the jug of hot water, she decided to take a look upstairs at her room. Tears came to her eyes as she looked at the fresh paint and the pretty floral wallpaper. The background was a fresh cream colour with large, bright coral flowers. She was touched that he had chosen to do this for her. She marvelled that maybe in his own strange way, he did love her after all.

Cilla started to get agitated so she went back down again to get the bottle.

Twenty-five

The wedding was only ten days away. Lily didn't have to do much, which suited her fine as the baby took all her time and energy. When she had been in hospital for ten days she hadn't realised how demanding it was. She wasn't so tired now, but a feeling of lethargy had come over her. It didn't feel right being in her parents' home again and although they had both been surprisingly nice, she was looking forward to the three of them moving into the house that Tom had found. She was pleased to find that it was in a pretty area, Greensborough, just outside of Tonbridge. A feeling of excitement went through her every time she wondered what the house was like. Before she went to sleep at night she would try to imagine herself, Tom and Cilla in a place that was theirs. The space to move around, the freedom to play music or make a mess or anything they wanted to do without any fear or apprehension.

Tom's cousin, Marg, had been very kind and helpful and she was coming to pick Lily up today and take her shopping for a dress to wear on her wedding day. Marg had also managed to get a pram from somewhere and she was bringing it in her station wagon. It would be so much easier when she could get out of the house with Cilla. She daydreamed as she looked out of the window into the cul-de-sac for Marg to arrive. It was one p.m. Cilla was asleep and her mother had agreed to look after her for two or three hours whilst Lily was out. Her mum and dad seemed to quite like having a baby in the house. She thought it was strange but it seemed to have softened them. Her father, particularly, didn't seem so angry all the time. She felt like laughing at the irony, considering that now she really had given him something to be angry about.

She saw a car pull up and could see it was Marg. Lily ran out to give her a hand with getting the pram out of the back. 'Hello, Marg!' She felt a bit awkward; she'd only met Marg once before about a week ago, but they had talked on the phone about wedding things and she could tell that Marg was a good person. They managed to get the shiny blue-and-white pram out between them. It was difficult as it didn't fold down like the latest style. It was large and solid, with big wheels. It looked very comfy and had good springs.

'Thanks, Marg. It will be fab to be able to take Cilla for walks in this.'

'I'm glad to help. My neighbour didn't need it anymore and said you could have it. They even offered to drive over with it in their van if I couldn't fit it in my car.'

They got the pram indoors and her father even got out of his armchair to give it the once over. Her mother cooed and said how much she liked it. They like it because it's old-fashioned, Lily thought. Even though it was late fifties or early sixties style, Lily liked it too.

'See you soon, Mum, Dad. Thanks for looking after Cilla. I hope she's good.'

Lily and Marg headed for the front door and escaped into the sunshine and into Marg's shiny, red Vauxhall.

'Let's get into Maidstone, Lily, and have a sit down with a cup of coffee and then we'll go looking for your dress. I've bought myself a lovely lime-green dress with a matching coat for your wedding,' said Marg, sounding almost as excited as Lily to be going on a shopping trip.

'That will look stunning with your dark hair, Marg.'

In no time they were wandering up Maidstone High Street in the late June sunshine and into Forte's café. Once they were comfortable in a high-backed booth and their coffees were on the table, Marg enquired how Lily was coping with everything. After talking about babies and her parents for a while, all Lily could think of was getting out into the shops and having some fun for a change. Fidgeting in her seat, Lily said, 'Can we go and look in the shops now? I'm so excited to be able to buy a normal dress again.'

Soon they were going from shop to shop. First Lily wanted to look in Martins, for old times' sake as much as anything. The clothes were gorgeous as they had always been but there was nothing suitable for the wedding. After a while of dodging around Saturday shoppers and looking in different shop windows, they came to Richards. Lily had always liked their clothes but they had been too expensive for her. They went in and looked anyway. The shop was elegant with a pale-blue, plush carpet and two gold ornate chairs in matching pale-blue velvet that looked too good to sit on. The changing rooms had pale-blue damask curtains swished back with gold ties.

Lily sorted carefully through every rack of dresses until she found a shift dress in heavy white lace. It was short, about three inches above the knee, sleeveless, and although it had a tiny stand-up collar, there was a keyhole cut-out below, discreetly covering her cleavage. It fitted her perfectly and even made her look slim. As Marg admired it they both knew they had found the right one. It was five pounds. While mulling over the cost, Lily stared into the window and her eyes focused on a beautiful wide-brimmed black hat on a mannequin. Unable to help herself, she rushed over and plonked it on her head and stood in front of the mirror.

'Ooh! That looks nice, Lily! Hats suit you. I love it with the dress. Come on, I'll buy the hat for you.'

Lily stared at her reflection. It looked really good. She looked like a girl of sixteen again.

'Thanks, Marg. Are you sure?' Lily was amazed at how kind Marg was and she hardly knew her. Marg gave her a quick hug and Lily disappeared back into the changing room. She came out and handed the dress to the well-groomed blonde assistant who gave her a smile and began to wrap it gently in white tissue paper.

She then put it into a large pale-blue paper carry bag with 'Richards' in gold lettering across it, with the hat already snuggly inside. Lily gazed around the shop once more. She thought she may not be back for a long time.

Once out in the warm sunshine again, Marg saw they were opposite Marks and Spencer. 'Let's go in here, I want to get something for me and Alf for dinner tonight then we can have a cup of tea in their café.'

They wandered around looking at all the tempting packaged meals, the neatly displayed vegetables and then the smorgasbord of desserts until Marg found what she wanted. Once her packages were in her shopping bag, Marg groaned. 'My feet are aching; come on, Lily, let's get some tea and sit down.'

Sipping the hot tea, Lily eagerly tucked into the Bakewell tart that she had chosen. It was big and delicious and had a glacé cherry on top. Lily was glad to take the weight off her feet; it was the most walking on pavements she'd done in months.

'What sort of cake do you want for the wedding, Lily? My mum's offered to make it.'

'That's very nice of her.' Lily looked at Marg, surprised. 'I just want everything to be really simple. I was thinking of just a love-heart sponge, iced and with pink rosebuds piped on. Would that be okay? I know it's not traditional but I don't much like tradition.'

Marg leaned across and squeezed her hand. 'That will be just fine. I'll tell her to make one for you.'

They walked out of Marks and Spencer and Lily bumped into Ralph, a mutual friend of hers and Jo's. 'Ralph! What a surprise. How are you?'

'I've been good, Lily. How are you? I hear you had a baby.'

'Yeah! I'm getting married in a few days. It doesn't seem possible, does it? Have you heard from Jo?'

'Congrats on getting married and no, I haven't heard from her much. Did you hear she got busted for drugs?'

'No! How did that happen? To my knowledge she never took drugs,' Lily answered incredulously. She couldn't believe her ears; there must be some mistake.

'She must have got in with the wrong crowd. They're sending her to a remand home.'

'What? You know she's having a baby too, don't you?'

'Yeah, I know, but she's been sentenced to six months. It's not right. She's too young for prison.'

'Ralph, if I write her a letter would you post it to her in an envelope addressed in your writing? Her mum won't let her have anything to do with me now.'

'Sure, send it to me and I'll send it on. Are you okay?'

'I'm okay; my baby is really beautiful. I've named her Cilla. Tom really loves me and we're moving into a house in Greensborough. This is his cousin, Marg.'

'Nice to meet you, Marg! You named your baby after Cilla Black?' Ralph sounded incredulous now.

'You know me, Ralph; I love all the singers with the sad songs.'

They laughed together and said goodbye.

As they walked back down to the car, Marg turned to Lily and said, 'Are you all right? You look like you've had a nasty shock.'

'I have. I can't believe she got into drugs. If they put her away for six months, she'll be having her baby in the remand home. It's crazy. Nobody deserves that.'

'He may have got it wrong, don't get too upset. Come on, here's the car. Let's get you home.'

Only when Lily climbed into bed that night could she be alone with her thoughts. Her mind had been racing ever since she had bumped into Ralph. The anger she felt towards Jo was still bubbling inside her; it had only been three weeks since Jo had landed her bombshell. As her rage threatened to rise up from where she'd put a lid on it and overcome her again, her concern that she had felt on hearing the news about Jo became submerged. Impulsively, deciding to write a letter to Jo, she sprang out of bed and found a pen and some paper.

Dear Jo,

I bumped into Ralph in Maidstone today and he told me your news. It's hard to believe. I don't know what happened, we never did drugs. I'm sorry that this has happened but I'm still angry with you and Tom for going behind my back. I expect you've heard that we're getting married next week. I'm not gloating like you did but for different reasons, this is the way it's turned out. The social worker says maybe you felt abandoned by me but I doubt it. You were probably glad that I shut myself off so that you could get him to yourself. I may have been stubborn but I still needed to know that you cared about me. I feel so hurt and betrayed by you that I can't find words to express it. God knows how it's all

*going to turn out but I doubt we'll see each other again.
I still care about you and I hope it's not true that you
have to go into a remand home. Hope you sort your
life out. We both have our babies to think about now.
Take care, Lily.*

Lily was sitting on the bed, hunched over the pad on her
knees. She re-read the letter. She knew she wanted to
spit out more venom towards Jo but hearing what was
happening to her, she just couldn't do it. Writing to Jo
helped but not enough to finally let go. Feeling weary, she
got under the covers again. Cilla made a little whimper
from her cot and Lily felt immediate guilt. She scolded
herself for being selfish and only thinking about herself.
She had to start acting more like an adult for her baby's
sake. If I think about my dress and the wedding, maybe
I'll fall asleep. Fresh anxiety gripped her. She had been
avoiding thinking of the future as Tom's wife and she
wasn't going to look at that now. One step at a time, that's
all I can do. It felt as if she was walking down a road
and just putting one foot in front of the other without
knowing where it was taking her. She only knew they both
loved Cilla and that was all that mattered. She finally
fell asleep, feeling that a higher force had taken over her
life and she would allow herself to go where it took her.

❁

The day of the wedding came. It was a hot and sunny July day. After feeding and changing Cilla, she had to wait for her turn in the bathroom. Then, carefully putting on her makeup, she added long, black false eyelashes to make her eyes stand out under the wide brim of the hat. They would be leaving in half an hour but she was ready. Cilla was ready too and she had just woken up from her nap. She looked very pretty in the tiny pink dress with rosebuds across the front. Both of Lily's aunties had come up from Hampshire and Aunt Mavis had offered to stay behind to look after Cilla. Lily was grateful; it would be difficult enough today without having her baby with her. Taking another look at herself in the mirror, she knew she looked nice. Tom would be surprised.

Going down the stairs carefully with Cilla in her arms she saw that her family were all ready. Her mother was looking very elegant in a navy blue dress and jacket and a big pink hat with pink feathers on the top. Her father was in his best blue suit and a white shirt with a blue tie. He looked reasonably happy and not so threatening. Simon looked extremely smart in a modern light-grey suit with a pink shirt and a thin grey tie. Sam was looking very grown up and proud of himself in a white shirt and long grey pants.

'You look nice, Lily!' said Sam straight away as she entered. He was the first to comment, which Lily thought was very sweet from an eleven-year-old.

She smiled at him. 'You look good yourself, Sam! You look really lovely, Mum. Dad and Simon have brushed up well.'

They all looked at Lily, seeming pleased with her praise and each returned the compliment, bar her father who was puffing on a rollup. Her thoughts switched to Tom and Carl and she wondered what they were going to look like. Tom had told her they were catching a bus to the wedding as there wasn't room for them both in Marg's car. Marg and her husband were taking Mrs Bennett. She was itching to get going and her family were just milling around the kitchen so she said, 'I think we should go now before any of us gets something on our clothes.'

They agreed this was a good idea and all headed for the front door.

'Aunt Mavis, thanks for staying here with Cilla,' said Lily. 'Her bottles are made up in the fridge. You know where the kettle is. The nappies and all that are in the big pink bag in the lounge room. I hope she's good for you. We'll only be a couple of hours.'

Aunt Mavis seemed to see that she was anxious. 'It's all right, Lily, don't worry. I'd rather be here making the sandwiches for when you all get back. I'm not one for social dos!'

Lily knew that was certainly true and stopped feeling guilty. Aunt Mavis had literally been stood up at the altar and had kept her wedding dress hanging in her room these last twenty years, just like Miss Havisham! She'd taken to smoking and drinking gin and tonics and had become a career woman working at the British Mint. Lily gave her a hug, noticing how thin she was and how tired she looked. Her sister, Aunty Anne, was quite the opposite, being a very tall, large woman. She had a son Simon's age from a romance in the war. Now she had 'Uncle' Colin in her life and they had got married a couple of years ago. Aunty Anne had stayed at home with her parents for most of her life.

They all piled into the two cars and got to Tunbridge Wells in twenty-five minutes. She was glad she'd elected to go in Simon's dark-green Triumph Herald with Simon and Sam. Her father tended to get very bad-tempered when driving and her mother and Aunty Anne could put up with him. She was stunned to see them all smiling when they got out of the car. Her father must have put on his jovial persona for Aunty Anne's benefit. Entering the beautiful, old sandstone building, Lily read the directory on the wall and led the way up the marble steps to the second floor.

The relief she'd felt was short-lived when she could see Tom wasn't there. She suddenly felt anxious. Thoughts flew into her head like, what if he's changed his mind? She looked around at all the eager faces, standing around chatting in the grey-carpeted hallway. Then, realising that everyone was looking forward to the day, all dressed up in their best clothes and there may not even be a wedding. Her heart sank. She thought she may be stood up like her Aunt Mavis. Maybe Tom had decided he prefers Jo after all. A chilling picture popped into her head of Jo making a last dash over to Tom's to persuade him that he would be better off with her.

As she chatted with family and friends she tried to keep the anxiety out of her face but couldn't stop looking at her watch. They had arrived a bit early but even so, it was only fifteen minutes before it was their allotted time at ten thirty. She glanced across at Tom's mum looking like candy floss in a pale pink dress with matching short jacket. She looked extremely happy and didn't seem to have noticed that her son hadn't arrived yet. Lily walked down the hallway towards the stairs, talking to people as she went and trying to look nonchalant as she edged nearer the window at the top of the stairs. As she looked around her, she felt that everyone there was a stranger. Her family, never close, were all dressed up for her wedding with a groom they had only met a couple of times. They had never met the groom's mother until a few minutes ago. There were friends that were fun but there was no real closeness, mainly due, she supposed, to her never being able to have friends at her home. But most of all, the boy she was supposedly about to marry, someone she had only had a brief amount of time with and didn't love, looked like he may not even show up! Sadness threatened to engulf her and tears pricked at her eyelids. Not now, not now, she prayed.

As she stood very still the realisation hit her: her dearest friend that she genuinely loved and felt at one with, no matter what, couldn't be there. The circumstances had made it impossible. Lily knew she had made her choices, her daughter above all else. In that love of Cilla, she shared a total bond with Tom. He had made choices too. A tear escaped as she felt the full weight of what they were about to do. She dabbed it with a finger so no-one would guess and looked again out of the window for Tom.

Minutes later, Tom, looking worried, ran up the stairs. Lily's shoulders relaxed as she took a step towards him. She leaned into him and whispered, 'What happened? I thought you weren't coming.'

He held her tight, looking into her eyes as if the very idea was crazy. 'I couldn't get Carl to get up and get himself ready. He 'ad too much to drink last night at the bucks turn and wouldn't budge. So I missed me bus and had to wait for the next one.'

Tom looked more flustered than she had ever seen him before. Her heart softened towards him. 'Is he coming then?'

'I dunno, he might still make it.'

Lily could tell how disappointed he was. Carl was his only brother and it was natural to want him there. She knew Mrs Bennett would be upset. 'Never mind, your mum and two cousins are here. We've got Kathy and her boyfriend, my friend Ivy and her boyfriend, the Higgs and most of my family. It will be okay, let's go in.'

Lily didn't really hear much of what was said. It was over in a few minutes. Tom put a wedding ring on her finger and kissed her. Everyone cheered and they all went out to the lawn into the sunshine so the next couple could go in. Tom whispered how beautiful she looked. For the first time in months she did feel beautiful. Looking around her she saw that everyone was looking happy, even her parents. She realised she felt happy too.

Her thoughts unbidden went to Jo once more. In her heart she wished Jo only happiness and wondered if perhaps they would be friends again one day. Tom whispered to her again. Bending her head gently to lean on his, she heard him say, 'Let's go home now to our beautiful daughter.'

Pamela Ann Sun grew up in Kent, England. She has fabulous memories of the music and fashion of the 1960's! Many Saturday nights were enjoyed with her best friend at the pub in Sevenoaks, watching great bands like The Kinks and The Hollies.

After marrying young and having two daughters, the family immigrated to Australia. The new life soon encouraged a passion for self-discovery, spirituality and natural healing. She now practices hypnotherapy and is a health counsellor.

The novel, *Big Dreams* is loosely based on true events.

Acknowledgements

Heartfelt thanks to my partner Denis for his ongoing support, emotionally and technically!

And to my daughters for their unwavering love and encouragement.

Also thanks to the friends who gave their time to give some wonderful input to the novel.

A big thank you to Julie Postance from iinspire media for all her patience with our consultations.

Thank you to my editor Anita Saunders for being so good to work with.

Thank you Jennifer from Fresh Vision for your wonderful artwork for my book cover.

And last but not least, thank you Nelly from PixBee Design for a stunning book layout.